SURRENDER

and other stories

SURRENDER

and other stories

a book of short stories by
Karl Hiltner

ИІЄМ$Т Ҡ РRESS

HUDSON

Copyright © 2021 by Karl Hiltner

Kniemst Press
Hudson, Ohio
www.karlhiltnerbooks.com

ISBN 979-8-9852154-2-7
Library of Congress Control Number: 2021923110

Contents

1.
Jim, Nell, and Kate

He turned the wagon from the field and the horses headed to the barn. They knew the way with loose reins and walked the path worn by the thousands of hoof prints shod with steel. The horseshoes came from the grandfather's blacksmith shop across the meadow and up the hill. Kate watched from the pasture. It was not her day to work. She was the only one of the three horses that could see, and she watched the big Percherons come up to the barn. It was Jim and Nell's day to work, both blind from the cruelty of their previous owner.

"Judas Priest," he cursed under his breath.

"Judas Priest," he cursed again out loud, blaming his young sons as if it was their fault that the cutter had not been properly sharpened.

All day the blades had been difficult to work with. Though he had tried to sharpen the steel throughout the day, it was a day when the heat warped the steel, or the toughness of the grassy stems or their moisture content caused the mowing and the cutting to be more difficult than usual. There was nothing that was usual and easy on this farm, and everything was difficult when you worked one hundred and eight acres by horse and hand, and had six mouths to feed.

Vernon did not suffer fools nor mechanical difficulties, and he cursed the wagon and the horses and the day as they moved towards the barn. Though he treated his animals well, he too, was a cruel man. And he cursed the day, and the wagon, and the blades, and his sons, and his daughter, his infant son, and his wife as he headed to the barn, and most of all the mother-in-law who was now at the farm from town for an afternoon visit in her goddamned Chevy coupe with the ahh-ooo-gah horn that she blew because it irritated him, as she made the corner on the Cooperdale Road and came up the lane to the house.

The somnolence of the August day wore on him, and he thought of the cutter repair, and the adjustments he would need to make before the mowing to be done the next day. The county contracts for limestone supply were coming due, more dynamite stocks and blasting caps needed to be purchased, and the star drills sharpened and tempered. The short one was used by the younger boy to start the hole in the limestone with the eight-pound sledge, and the older boy used the long drill to finish it with the twelve-pound hammer. There was always work to be done on the neighbor's machines when he was hired for a mechanical repair to rebuild a shaft or bearing, or to reseal a magneto assembly that leaked and fouled the contacts so that a spark could not be generated. But he could not consider the large black snake that lay in the grass warmed by the sun by the side of the barn that he did not see.

He could not be bothered with the un-hitching of the horses, though his sons were too young to lift off the collars by themselves unless one climbed onto the backs of the horses and handed them down to the other. And the bridles, and the reins, and the traces, and the single trees, and the double tree which all needed to be hung in the tack room beside the horse stalls. And the forking of the hay from the maul to feed the horses and also for the fifteen milk cows which would soon be led to their stalls and milked for the second time each day.

The boys followed from the fields behind the wagon, feet as tough as hooves, chewing on grains of wheat, or sucking on clover stems, dragging the rakes behind them, tines up so that they would curl over the grass, or bump across the stones on the path. The cows would need to be milked; the boy's day was not yet done. Fifteen milk cows gave fifteen gallons of milk twice a day that would have to be poured into the separator, one doing the pouring and one doing the cranking. The cream thus yielded was sold to the dairy, and the skimmed milk left over was mixed with wheat middlings and fed to the pigs. But first the older brother would have to climb to the rafters of the barn and thread the rope onto the pulley so that the hay could be lifted into the loft from the wagon bed. Somehow the hornets never bit him as the eleven-year-old balanced on the beam forty feet above the ground. There was seldom time for play, there was always much work to do.

There was not much joy and laughter on this farm, even since before they were born after their mother's father died. The boys did not know what a loveless marriage of convenience was, and they worked without complaint.

Big Jim stopped first, hitched on the right side, the lead horse and the strongest. He whinnied nervously, and jerked his head up against the bridle and the reins, and stepped his front legs up and down not moving forward or back, leaning back heavily on his great rear haunches. Nell picked up the scent and she stopped a half step beyond, now the double tree behind them angled forward left to right as the horses began to protest what they could smell but could not see.

Vernon snapped the whip angrily.

"Judas Priest," he scowled.

"Goddamn you, I'll beat the hell out of you too, if you don't pull this goddamned wagon into the barn," he yelled as he snapped the whip and cursed at the horses once again.

He was tired and angry and bitter, and the dust in his mouth made dry any patience that might have visited him earlier in the day. The horses could sense his bitterness and cruelty, but they could also sense what he did not yet see.

Vernon knew his animals and he knew how to make them work. They say he could walk through a herd at auction and pick out the best livestock. He knew how to put his boys and his daughter to work, and his wife who was born on this farm and who knew every inch of the land. But he could not always see everything. He knew that a horse had incredible senses that let them choose the way on a rocky path, or a rooted trail. He knew you could point a horse but not choose the places where they stepped. Now, four thousand pounds of blind horses pushed back against the wagon and would not obey and move forward. That was the worst thing you could do to Vernon, and he cursed the horses again and tried to drive them up the dirt ramp into the barn.

"Hee'yall, hee'yall," he coaxed, as he shook the reins against the backs of the horses, the gravelly curse directed to his stubborn charges.

"Git in 'ere, Jim. Git on in 'ere, Nell," he cried out and cursed at the Percherons.

The words came out from his throat like gravel violently washed from an overflowing stream during a storm.

When the horses reared, the left front wheel came off the ground, straining against the double tree crossed against it. Nell was no match for Jim though, as the big Percheron pushed back against her and she stumbled backwards against the bank of the ramp and when the left wheel met ground again it was because the right wheel came up and turned the wagon over. Now it was Vernon out of control, not the horses, and he was at the mercy of an upended wagon and four thousand pounds of horses who could smell but could not see the black snake that now moved through the grass and into the bushes that grew against the barn, and on out onto the bank by the creek, away from the trouble. He landed hard, the wagon toppled over him, partly covering him with hay, but the sideboards missed him as they flipped over and came apart and he lay stunned but not broken on the ground.

For a moment there was no sound, no cursing, and the boys rushed to pull their father free as he sat up and then let out another stream of curses and vitriol and invective before the oldest ran and grabbed the reins of the horses and pulled them free from the upended wagon. The horses whinnied and snorted, rearing and lifting their feet agitated with fear, away from the scent now, and they listened to the boy's voice. He held them loosely but firm like his father had taught him. Unafraid, the horses could feel the authority of the young master, and now the scent was gone.

Vernon stood up slowly, shook the hay and dust from his overalls, and slapped his straw hat against his legs as he got back to his feet.

"Judas Priest," he growled.

"Goddammit!" he yelled and he turned, limping slightly, stiffly, to walk up to the farmhouse.

"Git them goddamned horses into the barn and rake up this gad-durned hay!"

This day would be longer than usual, there were always the milk cows and the pigs, and hay to be put into the haymow and taken out to feed the animals. There was still plenty of daylight left and they knew their mother would keep their dinner, and that she would not talk about the incident when they came into the farmhouse. It was something that would never be talked about again in front of the father. At least the wagon would not have to be turned over. When it went over the low bank, it rolled back onto its wheels. Only the sideboards would have to be put back into place in the slats.

Big Jim and Nell were led into the barn and put into their stalls, and the younger boy ran to retrieve Kate from the pasture. There was still plenty of work to be done, it was just another day, and the boys did not have time to think about play.

2.
Charming

She did not know what to say, so she said yes. I had already made my own plans and did not want to waste a long flight over and back. After our work was done, I wanted to take advantage for a chance to spend a weekend in the city before I returned. So, when the company decided to send us both, she said she would come along with me to the city if I did not mind, for the weekend after we finished our work.

We were total opposites. My colleague was more conservative and religious, me only financially conservative and I liked to go to Mass at the diocesan cathedral because of the cantor. Still, I'd been to Israel and walked through the via Delarosa in Jerusalem, the holy lands of Nazareth, and had walked through the west bank in Bethlehem trying to find the Church of the Nativity, asking for directions from the people on the street. All I met were friendly despite the assassinations there the week before of two Palestinians by the Israelis, posters of martyrs to the cause everywhere. It was the historical stories in the bible that interested me, and not the later chapters of the New Testament where the stories became as strange as dreams. I believe that something happened in the desert four thousand years ago, and that something happened again two thousand years ago, but for me it was due to technology and a knowledge that we did not yet possess. I preferred priests who had taken a simple vow of humility and poverty, and liked less those who had amassed a proud and prejudiced wealth.

She had an innocence about her that was natural and very disarming, She leaned into her work in a certain way when she was thinking about something, as if she were entering the screen to become one with the computer. She was so smart she was sometimes dismissive of people if she thought their work was unhelpful. When she taught her Sunday School class, it amused her when the boys took notice of her, because they were young enough to still be innocent. And when her very tall and very large husband, who was a law enforcement officer entered the room to take her home from church, they liked her even more. But she was generally disappointed in men because her unmarried friends felt that all the good men were already taken, and all the ones who were even the slightest bit interesting were already divorced, or worse, still married but on the way to a divorce.

The project leaders were a disaster. There are still people who think that the more complex, the more impressive is the presentation. My company should have been able to hire the best and the brightest. It is the basis of everything successful everywhere. Over many years we were a world-wide talent draw. But you know you are in trouble when a page is filled with too many points and too many goals. Page after page of outlines is too much to retain, and the real work is always different than the presentation assumptions.

There were lots of pages to take with us, but it didn't bother my colleague. She was good at everything else that mattered, as well. That will get you good reviews, and a promotion.

We sat facing a window at JFK waiting for our flight out, and for the first time we had a personal conversation. I discovered a side of her that we always miss in other people unless we have the time and space to discover it. You do not need to like somebody to find the other side. Reporters and lawyers know this. It helps if you want to relax and get to know someone when it is not required by work or the law or fueled by drinks or drugs. Here was someone with a sense of adventure that you could not guess beforehand, someone who had seen famine in remote villages with her husband, risking disease and the lack of security to see it, feel it, and try in some small way to assuage it. Here was someone whose idea of vacation was not monuments and history, sun and sand; nor travel to expand one's ability to be falsely profound. She and her husband wanted to experience people and places with a past but with an uncertain future, those who possessed only a tenuous suffering present. I did not know what to say because I was taken aback by her candidness and matter-of-factness, and the risk taking that I had not imagined. Her experiences were simply said and factual without emotion, except there was a trace of weariness. We gazed out the window on the fleet of aircraft before us, one of which would take us through the skies over Europe.

We arrived directly from the airport, a quick drop off at the hotel, and on to the office. The formalities of old Europe were still evident in the hierarchy of topics and the individuals who presented them. It was going to be a long week. Things that were deemed necessary here had been eliminated without question back home decades earlier when 64kilobytes of RAM memory was state of the art. Here, there were formal legal requirements on data use and distribution that up to now had only required common sense discretional controls. At least the office attire was more casual as if it offset the organizational formality. But office doors were closed, not open. You had to knock to enter. So much for the transfer of culture or lack of it from our U.S. parent. It was like the difference between friendliness and civility. Here was a regimental lack of simplicity and individual initiative. It was evident in the way staff meetings took place. Before the boardroom door was closed you could see the assigned places at the table, and the way you took your seat and spoke on subject. You needed to go to the top, to get to the bottom. It was a long way down.

Midweek, we left the office early to sit together in the Gaffel across from the Dom, with a Kölsch in our hands and the two great towers rising beyond the windows. The formal facade of the office fell away. One colleague was quiet, he was in the midst of moving to a flat that he had intended to live in and raise a family. His fiancé had other ideas which did not include a child, after years of living in separate flats in the same building. Another was silent, private, and happily married. Another's wife was pregnant, and he wondered what his life would be like following the birth of their first child. The newest colleague among us was an immigrant learning the language to be able to receive a permanent residency.

The presence of Americans forced English at the table.

Looking out over the great Dom, I heard the only unsolicited comment on the war that I had ever heard spoken. The Allied bombings destroyed the Old Town and all the bridges spanning the Rhein, but the Dom was withheld from destruction with the exception of one errant bomb which penetrated the roof but did not explode. The errant bomb caused no irreparable damage.

"We were so stupid for what we did in the war," our blonde colleague said with sorrow, downcast eyes, and a slow shake of his head.

"We were so stupid."

There was no reply from anyone else after a pause in the conversation. Seventy years after the war was still not time enough.

Through the windows we could see the plaza of the Forecourt and the artists who needed to cover their unfinished chalk paintings for the night. The largest in-process work on the Forecourt was Rembrandt's De Nachtwacht, The Night Watch. At about half size to the original it was still very large, the figures almost life-sized. If you saw the artist away from his work you could not guess what he did for a living. He wore a white cotton shirt rolled up to his elbows, blue workman's overalls, black running shoes, a black baseball cap worn backwards, and hands stained from the chalks. You might think he had just come from an industrial shop floor. Here in this country, the shop floor was arguably more important than the office suite. Here there was no blue collar versus white collar, and what was designed and made in this country was important. He had a medium build, strong forearms and a strong neck. While he worked, he talked about art in a matter-of-fact way to all who visited and strolled through the Forecourt each day. He spoke in an accented English to the tourists, and switched back and forth in German as he communicated with local residents.

Our work had taken place at a historically important industrial site. If you walked down the central Allee you found yourself on a boulevard of plane trees with their dappled peeling bark. There were gardens and sculptures, fountains and pathways. It was a very pleasant stroll to the office if you had time to walk through the enormous site. It was still an industrial powerhouse, important to the world war effort seven decades earlier, but like all great companies in history, though still important, it was now only a reminder of what is once had been.

From the vantage point of the rooftop view from the highest building looking south, the Rhein was west to your right. Ship traffic plied this great working river which flowed north past one of the greatest cathedrals in the country on its way to the North Sea. On a clear enough day looking eastward, you could see the forested Bergisches Land region of the North Rhine-Westphalia state.

We had agreed to weekend together after our work was done, and now we drove north along the Rhein to the city I wanted to visit. We reserved rooms in the Altstadt-Nord on Machabäerstraße.

Restaurants line the Rhein River through the Old Town. Couples are everywhere on the walkways of the west bank of the river and in the parks along the way. Here in this city, one lives outside because that is where life is celebrated outside of small flats.

On Saturday, now that our work was finally done, we shopped for postcards, went to cafes, and took a rented car to a nearby palace. We managed to become lost on the way, and I had to make our way off of a walking street, reversing the car back off of the cobblestone walkway to return to a village street to get lost one more time along our way. Dinner was beside the river, a concert at the Cologne Philharmony, and afterwards we found a bottle of wine in a shop still open and carried it by the neck through the streets. We managed to open it and find a vacant bench overlooking the river. We were colleagues in a foreign place, that felt like home along the water.

In the morning during Mass in the great Dom, we experienced the music, the smoke of incense; the light of the windows filtered through ancient pigments, and the presence of the body and blood of real life in a city that rose from the ashes of war. From the steps of the Cathedral, a huge tower Finial was displayed beside us on the ground of the Forecourt, which at the top of the church appeared small when viewed from ground level. Beside us here, it was a stone carving unimaginably 10 meters tall. What had appeared to be small was still large.

We took one last walk through the Old Town, through the Hauptbahnhof, onto Domstraße, and to the street of our small hotel. We did not talk, but it was a pleasant walk, and the people on the street were enjoying a quiet day on this Sunday morning. We passed closed shops and open hotels on the way to our small pension. Along the way we heard a young girl's voice quietly singing under her breath, the sound barely audible, and at first, we could not see where it was coming from.

Then we saw her, a young girl unabashedly singing to herself as she walked along the straße. She did not realize that we could hear the quiet sound she was making, and the sweetness of the sound. I could feel the vitality of her youth, of years not yet lived which did not yet lay heavily upon her. For all of us there will be remembered the passage of time in our lives, of births and deaths, losses and regrets, and of war and peace, but there was none of that in the voice of that young German girl. She was two generations removed and did not experience or understand the destruction and rebuilding of a humbled city and great nation.

She was charming and innocent, and the guilt of the war had not touched her.

3.
The Last Shot Fired in Anger

He was the most gentlemanly of all the executives. He was unfailingly polite. During meetings he listened to what everyone had to say, even when you could sense his impatience, but he was always civil, especially if the person was at a lower management level than he was. He related to people well – up and down – but he may not have been taken as seriously, or perhaps the way to say it is, without as much attention as someone less polite, someone with more crude directness, though both be equally competent. I had witnessed many examples where the one less polite was the one who received more attention. He was not as loud as most of the men at his level. Nor even as much as the few women who would not have been there if they were not. He was just not as outwardly aggressive. The senior leaders knew him though, and recognized him. They knew that he was smarter than most, better educated, better read, and more cultured. For the best of the best that mattered as much as a man's performance, which was always a given at that level in the organization. Vic Marbolt always performed, and he always got an audience.

One of the executives to whom Vic reported liked to sit at his conference table before a meeting and go through the stock prices of his portfolio. He would call up a computerized voice service provided by his broker that announced his investments one by one, with the current market prices and the day's gains or losses spoken aloud. He liked to put the service on the speakerphone, and allow anyone who might be in the room to overhear. The list was long. He enjoyed listening to the prices of his stocks when he was between meetings. He sometimes did this more than once in a day.

This was during a year when virtually all stocks went up in one direction only, when our stock was considered more valuable than cash. If the company made an acquisition, stock was only offered for the best, highest quality deals, because our stock price, too, only went up. Cash was used for any second or third tier acquisition. And this was when cash still earned substantial interest, or could be loaned out at attractive rates for great, leveraged profit, using the cash thrown off from the existing businesses to fund greater and greater leverage. Eventually there would be a signal, and an indication of things to come, but for now we had enough hubris to declare stock swaps only for the best deals, not cash, and we still expected a doubling or tripling of our stock price and market capitalization.

If these stock price reports were put on the speakerphone, Marbolt would leave the room. He had no patience for such displays of egoistic behavior. During breaks I liked to remain and listen, entertained by the results of market forces. Our GM, who was a few years younger than Vic, enjoyed showing off his investments while he checked his emails and worked his thumbs on his Blackberry. The speakerphone droned on in an attractive female voice. I didn't mind that voice at all.

The general manager knew that Vic had no patience for this behavior despite the enjoyment it afforded himself. The truth was that he hoped to own as elegant a home in the best neighborhood as the one that Marbolt already owned. It was a home where many of the city's best society were entertained, an elegant home of slate, and brick, and stone – built when the city was still a Fortune 500 powerhouse. Vic owned an architectural gem where he lived with his devoted wife of social standing and her own executive ability, and three beautiful children.

The searing sun slanted oppressively in the western sky and brought no relief from the heat and the humidity as it headed toward the horizon. There was always the smell and always the sun. It was there when you deplaned in Tan Son Nhat, you could not escape it once you arrived, and for the rest of your life you could never be free from the memory of the smell of Vietnam. It was the odor of unceasing humidity – human, and animal smells – the smell of water and foods and feces, of water close to the surface of the soil, of putrid decomposition and teeming life mixed with the diesel fumes of ever-present mechanized warfare.

"The sunlight is still hitting my eyes," Vic thought as he stood atop this paddy dike with the sun blinding his eyes twice done, as he talked to the Lieutenant from Texas.

"Our forward action is over and we have returned to our outpost. I am standing on the dike mounded up between two rice paddies. There is no escaping the sun, and when it is at a certain height above the horizon it reflects off the water a second time, blindingly so. The water and the sun are everywhere."

He suddenly thought of another, later life.

"I am with a business colleague standing on a hillside at Balaton above the lake on firm, sandy soil."

It is said that the northern shore of Lake Balaton is perfectly situated by an accident of geologic history that causes the sun to shine doubly on the grape vines which cover every hillside of the northern shore. In much the same way it had done in Vietnam, a half a world away. At Balaton the sun hit the grapes once from the sky above, and a second time from below with the reflection off the water.

"I don't know why it's made me think of this again, perhaps the colleagues who arrived from Hungary with their Budapest suits. I need to make sure there are no comments on their dress.

We don't wear red polyester suits here, but no mind. These cultured men speak languages, know history, have suffered want of things we take for granted, like ever present oranges or bananas, fruits that used to be available only on certain holidays of the year unless you were a party boss, or had access to travel or to those who did."

The next meeting was about to begin. Vic and I had to present our case for declining the acquisition that the younger GM wanted badly to do. He was still thinking stocks and prices while the speaker phone droned on, and he wanted to move forward with a deal which he hoped Vic and I would recommend at the conference table.

I went through the financial model, the assumptions, growth rates, prices, costs, required investments, inventory, base costs, and the cannibalization potential against our current products and services. The EBITDA generated by the inputs to my model did not come close to the accretive gains the GM expected. The deal would not generate enough cash flow, and it is, and always is, about the cash. As a stand-alone business the potential acquisition had struggled along, and it was an available target, but when restructured with our business, the value would not be there. Vic and I could not recommend the deal. The synergy with our products was real, but it would only be an extension of what we were already doing or what we planned to do. It did not bring enough to the table to justify the required price. At least not for our company, a company the street was not yet betting against. That would come later, unexpectedly, and nearly take us down.

The meeting was over. The general manager told us we needed to find something else if this deal was not going to be the one. We had to find another. He said he needed to call his broker before his next meeting began. Vic and I left the conference room. If we were not going to do a deal and buy this business, the GM would at least add to his own personal portfolio.

"Only because the light blinded me," thought Vic, again back at the rice paddy.

"It is only because I was facing the sun, letting the Lieutenant talk to me with the sun to his back."

"Vic," I said, "what do you want me to do?"

"Take one more look. Make sure we did not miss anything."

"Let me do some more analysis on this one, but I just can't make the numbers work with the assumptions you gave me. I'll make some scenarios for you to look at which might make the numbers work. You'll have to decide which levers can work in the market. We can't recommend something that doesn't make sense, but I know we have to show some progress towards making a new growth acquisition."

"That's correct. Organic growth alone won't be enough to satisfy the street or the chairman."

"When are we going to meet with Ferenc to review the new product plans for our factory at Nagyvarászló?"

I knew that Ferenc was going to tell us that there was no problem with the space needed for the expansion. He was our most experienced factory director and he would also say there was plenty of component capacity for final assembly. He wanted to review with us the discussions he had already had with Tibor and Imre from the partner factories. It was early in the history of our joint venture partnership, and there was still unbounded enthusiasm within our team.

Ferenc owned a weekend house at Balatonfüred, with grape vines and a small wine cellar. Vic and I knew that Ferenc would talk about the latest harvest and how the barrels were aging, and how the splendid light reflected off the great freshwater lake. He would bring everyone a bottle of his new wine.

Vic began to think again of the sun and the reflection off the water, and he was back with the sounds and the smells of the jungle and rice paddies, of beasts of burden groaning in the heat, and the nasal throaty sound of the native language. The gentle sounds of leather straps and harnesses came back to him, of men, women, and animals moving through the sucking sounds of water and mud, and the ever-present explosions and gunshots in the distance, muffled by the thickness of the humidity which enclosed and suffocated everything.

The last day came for him, cruelly, 16June1971, with the 198th Infantry Brigade at Quảng Ngãi Province. 2nd Lt. Vic Marbolt's platoon engaged an enemy firefight. The incoming rounds of automatic weapons fire slapped against the leaves and the branches and the trunks of trees, spit into the earth, and cracked and hissed through the fetid air. An AK47 was less accurate than the M16, but when its slower and heavier caliber bullet tumbled in the air and entered your body it could follow the length of a bone if it slap-hit just right, not just penetrating but sliding the length of a bone inside your body, tearing the flesh as it went. The radio operator saw it happen. The bullet entered Vic's right arm at the wrist, shattering the scaphoid bone and followed up the concave anterior surface of the forearm radius. It tore through the cap of the humerus at the elbow and slid up the bone before it exited halfway to the shoulder just missing the brachial artery. The exiting bullet hit the stock of his M16, instead of embedding itself into his chest, and it saved his life. The rifle fell to the ground as Vic's hand involuntarily released its hold on the pistol grip. His body began to buckle from the shock of the impact as it spun him around onto the ground.

"It's funny," Vic remembered to himself, the strange thing that crossed his mind as he struggled against shock and unconsciousness.

"I will never again be able to wear short sleeve shirts in public."

It would be the last time he fired a gun in anger. Had it hit the artery and shredded it, or hit him in a hundred other ways he may have died instantly or bled to death before the chopper evac came, and surely could have cost him his arm or his life. He would never again fire or own a gun for the rest of his life.

The meeting began, and the general managers of Product Management, Sales, Engineering, and Operations all gathered around the conference table to review the new product capacity expansion proposal for the European operations.

"Vic, great tie," the sales leader said.

"You are really looking good today. Christ, you are a walking advertisement for GQ. I guess we're not formal enough for you here. Even in this goddamn overheated conference room you wear a formal shirt and cufflinks," he sneered.

"Can't we get the goddamned air conditioning fixed?" another complained.

"Don't give him a hard time, Chuck. He works well with the customers and you know that they appreciate him. He's got the best hand-made shirts in this room, and he puts us all to shame."

"Jesus, Vic, you really never do show a wrinkle," laughed the younger general manager.

The younger GM had requested and received both undergraduate and graduate school deferments before they did away with the draft and ended the war.

Vic just laughed and said he could give them all a little sartorial advice.

"All right, let's cut the crap and get started," growled the Operations leader.

"Lay off Vic, assholes."

He was a former army artillery officer who froze his butt off in Korea manning gun emplacements in bitter temperatures, the only other military veteran in the room.

Ferenc opened a satchel with pride and brought out bottles of his own white wine, enough for each of the executives seated around the table. Attached to each bottle was a small handmade label that said:

Baltonfüred Fehérbor
Az Háza Ákos Ferenc

"The sun was especially good to the grapes last year," he said as he passed out a bottle of wine to each of the executives seated at the conference table.

"Gentlemen, before we talk numbers, here is a gift for you to take home tonight."

"Enjoy, with pleasure!"

The meeting concluded. Vic and I went back to his office to sit at his work table and talk. There were no papers on the small table which was only large enough for two people to sit together and work. To its side was his large mahogany desk and cadenza. A neat blotter lay on top, phone, a desk pen set, wooden trays one on each side for incoming and outgoing papers, a Wall Street Journal folded on the right edge of the desk, and facing his chair on the left side of the desk a formal picture of his wife smiling into the camera. Behind on the cadenza were framed pictures of his children taken in the back yard of his elegant home. On the wall was a landscape lithograph provided by the company, appropriate for an executive of his level, and framed commemoratives of previous positions held. Product samples lined the windowsill.

The entire physical sum of a man's career can be held in an executive's office. The inner life and the sum of experience can seem to fill an entire conscious mind, sometimes finding expression in the face through scars, wrinkles, the shape of the mouth, the set of the eyes, and the way a man carries himself. But a man's unconscious mind can dream unbound, reaching towards infinity, and we talked quietly about our families and life.

He was back again on the dike of the rice paddy with the Texas Lieutenant. A few weeks later Vic would be wounded and evacuated, but on this day the war was not yet over.

"Now it is hitting my eyes," he thought as he stood atop the paddy dike.

The sun blinded his eyes twice, once from above and once from below as it reflected off the water.

"I am talking to the Lieutenant from Texas," he remembered.

Vic was looking away from the table where we sat together. I said something to him. We were through with deals and cash flows and target acquisitions for the day, and he suddenly began to talk about a Lieutenant from Texas.

"The sun was low in the sky, and I was talking to another Lieutenant about our families. We were standing on an earthen dike between two rice paddies. He was from a Texas family with a long line of men in military service."

"The sun was blinding me."

"I moved to stand in his shadow so that I could see his face. I heard the sound before I heard the crack of the shot, a sickening sound of metal crushing skin, bone, tissue, and blood, and I felt something pass close by my head that escaped from the Lieutenant with an infinitesimal whoosh. His face disappeared against the explosive impact and exit of the bullet, and the sun sprayed red against my eyes."

"A sniper tried for a double head shot as we stood together on top of the dike with the sun in my eyes in deference to the Texas Lieutenant. In the moment I moved to shade my eyes with his shadow the shot was made. He collapsed and I survived. I caught him in my arms and he died."

"He died with the sun shining on him as he lay in my arms on the dike, the sun shining on him from the sky above and from the reflection of the water below."

"A few weeks later I fired a gun for the last time in anger, and the war was over for me."

4.
Tecumseh

We called the old hermit, "Tecumseh," after the leader of the Shawnee nation. This was an Indian name we could easily pronounce. We did not know that his ancestor of two hundred years ago was called Koguethagechton, nor could we have ever pronounced it correctly. And we did not know that Netawatwees, the Lenape Delaware chief who preceded him, founded Newcomer's Town, before Koguethagechton founded Goschachunk at the junction of the Walhonding and Tuscarawas Rivers when the Great Council moved there. Our school only taught that this Indian village was destroyed by the colonial army in 1786 before it became the Coshocton that we knew.

In the time before the settlers came, five of the six Indian villages here were of the Lenape Delaware nation except the one Shawnee village along the Little Wakatomika Creek, near the Neldon Place, purchased by one of the early settlers only a generation after the last Indian left the township. Neldon was one of the first white settlers in the area. Stories were still told and retold of the early days, when Indians and settlers both were killed and revenge took place on both sides. There were stories of white men who hated the Indians so much that they would try to kill any that they met, hard men, some of whom could raid an Indian camp, kill and retreat, and who could reload a flintlock rifle on the run so as to be able to turn and shoot any Indian that followed, to avoid being killed and scalped himself.

Now Wakatomika is nothing more than a few houses at the intersection of a country road, and an Indian word that we liked to repeat because of the way the syllables rolled off our tongues.

But in 1774 it was important enough to be destroyed during Lord Dunmore's war before the beginning of the American Revolution, like all the other Indian villages that would be destroyed in later years. It was not far from the general store in Tunnel Hill to which we traveled in a two-horse wagon across the dirt packed country roads, through farmlands which lay on either side, some still owned by the descendants of the early settlers with names like Neldon, Preston, Gault, Buxton, McFarland, Fry, Lee, Pigman, and Doddridge.

We only knew that Tecumseh's long-ago ancestor, Koguethagechton, later called Captain White Eyes by the soldiers and settlers, was in fact a Delaware, not a Shawnee chief, who was born before the time that Coshocton became a town for white settlers. We did not know Tecumseh's real name, and we talked about the Indians who used to live on the land we now occupied, and the lands back east in Pennsylvania from where the Indians had come. They were crowded out by the settlers who had purchased their homesteads from the government on Indian land that the government had forced them to give up. The move west to Ohio was only the first of many moves that the Indians would be forced to make, from Pennsylvania to Ohio, then to Indiana, then to Missouri, and finally to Kansas and Oklahoma.

We knew only that the hermit lived in an ancient log cabin, made of stacked logs un-notched at the ends in the old Indian style, though there was now a rough chimney on the side of the cabin. The opening in the center of the roof for a central hearth was closed long ago. No white man would live in such a place. We did not know if he was a real Indian, but he was allowed to keep to the old cabin in the woods, and he performed odds and ends for the Doddridge family who still owned the land on which he lived. They had lived in this part of Ohio since the first white settlers came here, also come west from

Pennsylvania as had my family, seeking land for farms without close neighbors.

It was said that Tecumseh came back east again to Ohio from the Delaware Reservation in Oklahoma, a hundred years after the last Indian had left these parts, fifty years after the War of the Rebellion ended. We did not know why or exactly when he returned, and neither the Doddridge's nor my family ever talk about it. If we walked close by the woods in which he lived on the way to our one room school, we sometimes caught a glimpse of him sitting by the cabin door, on a bench made of a split log with short, rough-cut legs whittled from hickory branches thrust into four holes bored into the round bottom of the log. He neither retired from our view nor spoke as we passed by, and we did not linger longer than our gazes allowed. His skin was darker than ours, but not as dark nor ruddy as we imagined it should be. We did not know if it was a sooty darkness from the crude hearth of his cabin, or a roughness and hue tanned from the sun, or whether it was really the skin of an Indian. His eyes were dark and they may have been black, at least as far as we could see or imagine. He was simply the hermit we called Tecumseh, and although he had never given us a reason to be, we were all afraid of him. Despite our curiosity, we kept our distance from him.

It is easy to assign greatness to a man who is dead and who is no longer able to defend himself with the truth. That was certainly the case when Chief Koguethagechton, called Captain White Eyes succumbed to smallpox, according to the report from the military garrison at Fort Laurens where he was said to have died in 1778. Captain White Eyes, the peaceful leader of the Delaware Indians, was a friend of the new nation and of settlers and missionaries. He was both a friend to the Fort Laurens military garrison which guarded the new frontier from the British, and to the Indian chiefs who aligned themselves against the white settlers and new Americans. He tolerated and helped protect Moravian missionaries who attempted to Christianize the Delaware nation, and more than once had defended and protected the religious whites from attacks by Indians who did not accept the white religion. He protected the missionaries without prejudice from harm, but he himself was never accepted with a fullness of grace by the white race, most of whom considered all Indians, savages.

Captain White Eyes understood the superior technologies of the whites, anticipated the unending flow of settlers that were to come, urged his people to prepare for the inevitable change, and encouraged the Christian religion among his tribe. When he died, he was mourned not only by his own people, but tributes came from the white world's religious and military leaders. The distrust of other chiefs who had called for war against the whites, would not be validated until many years later, with the truth that White Eyes had in fact been betrayed and murdered by those same whites who had praised and mourned him – a murder made necessary if the Indians were to be forcibly removed from the land with a lack of leadership, and with as little resistance as possible.

There would be no new Indian leader to replace Chief White Eyes, there would be no time to replace the great Indian leader who had held the respect of both races as events began to cascade and lead again to the forcible removal of the weaker race from this part of the Ohio country. There would be no need of a public denouncement, no justification nor debate against the trusted, respected, native friend. The killing of an Indian was too easily accomplished. The value of a savage life paled in comparison to the efficacy of the inevitable march west. There could be no compromise with a native culture for whom fences were unnecessary, and whose language had no words for intangible laws, commercial organizations, and precepts of legal ownership.

Even before the moment the congress land of Ohio was surveyed by John Mathews in 1803, before the first white settlers arrived to the county, there could be no giving back to the Indians possession of the lands on which they had lived for millenniums. In less than twenty years the last Indian would be removed from the Ohio land forever, until the stubborn and hermetic return of Tecumseh, the presence of whose ancestors still appeared in the overturned soil of a plowed field each spring. The smooth surfaces of arrowheads and stone and flint tools dried in the sun of my family's section twenty field where the Delaware's had once made camp, and upon which now we farmed the land.

The laces on the engineer boots I wore reached well above my ankles, halfway to my knees. I crossed fields and fences to the one room school I attended, and the boots protected my shins and ankles from the scrapes and splinters that I experienced when I went barefoot through the fields and crossed the fences in the summertime. The old township road that followed the lane to our house was still passable by horse and wagon, though it was a rare passerby except for the mailman who carried the mail in a saddlebag and delivered it by horseback along the trail that split our north and south fields along the section lines. Life was sunup to sundown, lived with the rhythm of the seasons, the crack of a rifle or shotgun that filled our salted crocks with meat. It was the gathering of buckets of blackberries and the gathering of bushels of apples from the old gnarled orchard, grown from the saplings sold to settlers from one of the John Chapman nurseries, owned and planted by him when he crossed this land a century before, and was known as Johnny Appleseed.

Only one time did I have any interaction with the old Indian, and it was unintended, on a hot, barefoot summer day, on a horse I finally broke that almost broke me. I was lucky that day, when I first rode the only horse that we owned that was not a work horse, and that we kept not to ride but just to keep. It was the only animal my father ever owned which did not work or which was not raised for slaughter. He never explained why, it just was, an old Morgan that he bought and pastured in a rented field we used for hay that abutted the woods of the Doddridge place, and out over which Tecumseh could see the line of trees which followed the Winding Fork Creek to the southwest, five miles from the Little Wakatomika Creek which flowed to the east.

A twelve-year old boy who is used to plowing with horses feels an impatience and an attraction to a horse that just is, and is never ridden. The old Morgan, Brownie, had no saddle, just a rope bridle so that he could be led about when he needed to be brought from one field to another. I brought him to a fence post at the bottom of the field, and climbed onto his back, held the rope reins of the bridal and knitted my fingers into his mane. I held tight to a willow switch in my right hand that I had been carving to make into a whistle. There was no bit. Brownie started to buck and tried to throw me off, and began to gallop along the fence line at the bottom of the field, but I had control of his head and forced him up the hill and I began to strike him with the whip. I whipped him all the way to the top of that hill. By the time we got to the line of woods at the top, Brownie was so spent he could barely walk, and I saw that Tecumseh had stood up to watch the spectacle of boy against horse. When I saw him, he sat back down again without acknowledgement. That was the only time I ever had any interaction with the old Indian. There was never a word spoken between us before, during, or after. And neither did I ever have trouble with that Morgan horse again.

I would not know until the end of my own life, when I had given up all that I possessed and was left with only my thoughts and memories of a world that no longer existed, a world that began of farms and fields and horses, and ended with war and then the modern world, what it was to imagine what Tecumseh had felt, watching the boy that I had been, and the unbroken Morgan horse, and the war between the two of us on that hill.

"I, Tecumseh, of the Lenape Delaware Nation, have returned to native lands now not my own. I am descended from the murdered Chief of the Delaware Turtle Tribe of Peace, Koguethagechton, Captain White Eyes, whose squaw, Rachel Doddridge, a white woman captive, was also killed by the whites. She mothered and raised me, their son, George Morgan White Eyes, namesake of a President with the strength of a cavalry horse. I am descended from them, and from all the sons of all the reservations that followed."

"I, Tecumseh, the end of all sons, have returned to die in the Ohio land of my own GreatFather of two hundred years ago."

5.
Chloé and the Little Mermaid

In Copenhagen, the Little Mermaid sits by the water at the end of the Langelinie Pier. If you arrive at Copenhagen Kastrup, and have a long enough layover until your next flight, you can leave the airport and take a bus to town where it drops you off at a tourist information office near the Church of The Holy Ghost, the Helligåndskirken, on Niels Hemmingsens Street No. 5. We were on our way to the States, and I translated the name of the church for my two Hungarian colleagues into, "Szentlélek templom." From there it was only a twenty-minute walk to the statue of The Little Mermaid, the Lorelei, perched on the rocks by the water of the channel which joins together the Baltic and North Seas.

I was reminded of another mermaid that day by the harbor, a recollection of many years before, lured to a dissimilar place for my education, according to my mentor and married friend, Diane. It was not for my destruction against the rocks, nor for any moral or physical dissipation. From the time she found me young, alone, and uncomfortable at an office party, and invited me to help retrieve a special smoking device for her husband from their penthouse condominium several floors above, she decided that she needed to educate me, and I became her project.

That was how she found me at the beginning of our relationship. She asked me if I had ever seen a penthouse, and took me to her apartment to help her retrieve a long glass tube for her husband. In the elevator going back down to the party she pulled open the top of her low-cut stretch fabric dress and exposed herself to me wearing no underclothing, without the slightest inhibition of modesty. She partially hid the long tubular device inside the top of her dress, making sure that I had seen her. She watched me as she did this, looking up at me and not taking her eyes off my face while she tucked the device into the top of her dress.

Much later, after and near the end, she would tell me that where I had come from represented something wholesome and fresh, especially after the time she insisted to meet my mother and father. Something about the kind of woman she imagined my mother to be. Something at odds with the weariness, deceit, deterioration, and destruction of the world she described of the eastern seaboard from which she had come, a collapse of faith that encompassed the loss of familial closeness, understanding, and happiness. I did not understand this then, I was only able to see the external reality of her affluence, cars, prestige, and social status. I did not see the sorrow of a young daughter for a father lost to the horror of his own self-destruction, and the search for love to replace him, from a place where love had been lost. The closer we became, the more I did see the sorrow. I did not know that it would move from grief and then to despair until love intervened. But that would be another story.

Interesting people were always dropping by the large old Victorian house that she and her husband had purchased after they left the penthouse suite. The glass, steel, and concrete of their penthouse apartment no longer suited their growing family of three. They lived close to the university, and there was always a medical resident walking through the front door for dinner, a graduate student in history, a researcher of the new computer science field, or the journalist neighbor who had been a professor at a southern university, and who now added a southern charm to the northeast hospitality of Diane's inner-city townhome.

That is where I met Drew, an acquaintance from the athletic department with whom I would become a good friend. We played tennis matches with such energy and power that students at the university would stop to watch us play. He had escaped both his childhood and the city where he grew up, and told of the time he placed his finger into the bullet hole in a dead friend's chest from the shots that were fired at them by the police. It was years before he would attend, by the grace of a determined mother and a case worker who never gave up, a prestigious prep school, and then an Ivy League university.

Bread was always piled high on plates at the table, but not the kind of sliced bread my mother had served, this from a neighborhood bakery with a sinewy richness which you had to pull apart to eat. And I had never tasted the kind of chicken soup that Diane cooked for hours on the old kitchen's gas fired industrial sized cooktop at the back of the house. It was boiled whole in a huge stock pot which she then set directly on the table, having simmered with whatever fresh vegetables she had found at the market that day, placing only the large ladle inside with which you measured out your steamy meal. It was a stew that when you ate it you had to be careful about the bones that settled to the bottom, nothing tidy or pre-cut here like the food with which my mother had set our table. There was always enough to eat for everyone who came to table at dinner time. There was often someone new whom she had just met and was now welcomed to her home. This was authentic food, rich and natural, and so was every person who was seated around her table.

The kinds of people that came to her home were different from other friends and acquaintances I had known. Diane was the most sociable person I had ever met. Anyone with whom she worked or from whom she purchased any of her needs became her friend. Her house was open until late into the night for old friends and for those who would become new ones.

On this particular night, there was music on the radio, and the song was about a woman who needed to find love, she just wanted to find her man. There were five of us at the table which Diane had set that evening. It included James the medical resident, Richard a corporate purchasing agent, and Paul his friend who was new to the table, and myself. Diane's husband would join us later before the dinner broke up. Suddenly, Paul began to sing along with the music, totally uninhibited by the new friends to which he had just been introduced. He then lit a joint and passed it around the table. That was the start of the party.

Diane decided that after dinner we should go to a place across the river and continue our impromptu celebration. She insisted that we all meet her friends that owned a bar there. She took me aside and told me that it was a hooker bar, and that it would be part of my education to go there with the friends with whom we had sat at her table. The medical resident took a last hit but declined, he wanted to go into the library off of the dining room and sleep for a couple of hours before he started his rounds. Her husband declined, as well – he had some reading to do for his firm before a meeting with investors in the morning. That left the agent and his friend, along with Diane and me. Her sports car normally had only room for two, but somehow the four of us climbed into the car with its tiny back seat, and we set off for the bar on the other side of the river.

The Mermaid was off of a side street, a small place with a square bar in the middle of the room served from inside the four sides of the bar. An old-fashioned neon sign hung above the entrance with a nautical theme. It looked like it had been there for the three decades since the war. A few tables surrounded the bar and a stairway led upstairs. It was four miles to the Navy yard from Diane's home on the opposite side of the river, seventy miles up the river from the bay.

Diane introduced us all around to her friends who owned the bar, Aunt Joan and her husband Tom. He wore the biggest gold ring I had ever seen, and he let his wife do the talking to Diane and all of us after he said hello, then he continued with the business of the bar to serve his customers.

The same song played again on the radio that we had heard earlier in the evening at dinner, and Paul began singing again to no one in particular.

"I just want to find my man!" he sang and put his arms around his friend Richard and kissed him.

Richard sat beside him passively while he waited for his drink.

Diane ordered a glass of red wine for both of us, and she and Aunt Joan continued a conversation about the upcoming party at the Centennial Hall. Tom poured our drinks then turned back to the bar to discuss the offerings with another customer.

There was a large woman seated a few seats away from us at the bar holding an intense conversation with a large well-dressed man. He had a huge barrel chest and close-cropped hair and wore a fine gray woolen suit, a brilliant white shirt and silk tie, and a matching pocket square. The woman wore a very wide brimmed southern style hat with a red silk ribbon tied around the crown which descended off the back of the hat to rest on her shoulder above her well-endowed décolletage.

Lights shown and reflected off the wine glasses hung by their stems above the bar and created a sparkling effect for those sitting there. Music was still playing, Paul was still singing about his man, and the reflected light flashed off of Tom's huge gold ring. Diane leaned over to me and slid her arm around mine as we took a sip from our wine glasses, red, which Tom had poured for both of us.

"Hello Darling," she said as she squeezed her arm against mine and looked up into my eyes.

"Aunt Joan owns this place," she told me.

"Not her husband Tom, not any of it," she said.

"But he helps her run it, and he keeps it under control."

She raised the glass to her lips and moved closer to me. I could feel the warmth of her body and the faint sweet smell of red wine from her lips as she spoke.

"She takes care of the business end of things, and he takes good care of her."

Paul was still singing about finding his man, face flushed and now standing beside his chair, a bottle raised in his hand to no one in particular, both high and now drunk. He finished the song and put his arms around Richard to give him another hug, then kissed him again on the mouth and sat back down as if he were lost. He stared straight ahead at nothing, without emotion. Diane leaned into me and continued.

"That is Chloé with the wide brimmed hat."

"Her specialty is oral sex," she continued, "and if the two of them agree on a price," referring to the large well-dressed man with whom Chloé was earnestly speaking, "they will leave the bar and go upstairs."

Then she pouted the fullness of her lips in the way she always did when she finished telling me something important, and she raised up her eyes beneath her long lashes to look into mine. Taking my hand in hers, she smiled and kissed my fingers.

"Oh, Darling," she whispered into my ear.

Diane said these things about Aunt Joan, Tom, and Chloé as matter-of-factly as if she were standing in front of the stove in her kitchen, stirring a pot of chicken soup and telling me what she had just put into it.

"It's part of your education," she said to me.

Chloé and the large well-dressed man got up from the bar. He carefully took her hand and together they climbed the stairs to the second floor.

"Darling, let's not think about it anymore," she said moving closer against me, "it's just something you needed to know."

She called out to Aunt Joan and Tom to say that we needed to get back across the river to the city. She stood up and put her arm around my waist. Paul and Richard stood up from the bar and went outside to wait by the car, while Diane said goodnight to her friends.

"John has to go out of town tomorrow," she said to me as we left the bar and walked to the car.

"He'll be grateful if you can stay over and keep the child and me company in the house while he's away. It will be quiet, just the three of us, there won't be anyone else for dinner, and we can go to bed early and get a good night's sleep."

6.
The New Foundation

Troy Anderson was the most aggressive manager with whom I ever worked. He was not a large man, being only of average height and somewhat overweight. It is what happens to a man who works a sedentary job and who exercises too infrequently. He was a few inches less than six-foot tall but carried at least thirty pounds more than he should have. He was not in shape, and at forty-nine years old, he was beginning to pack on serious weight with the years, and his knees already hurt. He was just newly arrived to work at our office in Atlanta when he had a health scare of an embarrassing note, potentially deadly, but as it turned out for him it was a false alarm. It was only a momentary embarrassment, and perhaps fittingly so, affecting it was rumored, a delicate part of his anatomy, the use of which he referred to frequently in oaths against others who crossed him.

This from a man who once boasted, "I don't get heart attacks, I give heart attacks."

He was very humble for a few days after this health concern, but he soon forgot all about it, and his true nativistic nature re-established itself. It was apparent that he had not paid attention to his diet for some years now, you could see the red meat damage on his unexercised physique, with the added menu of French fries and years of high-fructose corn syrup sodas, though now an ever-present diet cola graced his desk. At least he managed to trade the high-fructose corn syrup for artificial sweeteners. His jowls were beginning to loosen when he spoke, and if you watched him eat, you could imagine the extra space they afforded for the food he ingested and enjoyed. But he still had a full head of dark brown hair, almost black just beginning to show a trace of gray at the temples. His small, sharp, dark, deep-set eyes were too close together for the size of his large head, and his aquiline nose was too delicate for the size of his face. Thin, unsmiling lips, all together with his smaller stature, added a menacing, sneering, almost rat-like quality to his face.

When he walked by or approached you, he always seemed to be leaning slightly forward, perhaps because of the shifting balance of his weight. His shoulders rounded into his arms as if he were always ready to reach out and take hold of someone. I am sure it was a display of unintended aggressiveness, but he couldn't help himself. He would get caught up in the emotions of things like the way introverted people do without intending to. Not at all reassuring, he had a hidden passive aggressiveness.

Despite his adult professional success, he was raised as a boy who always had to worry about money. He had grown up much less affluent, but now he was a man who enjoyed the comforts he had been able to obtain. It meant that, still always careful with money, he nonetheless enjoyed what he could now well afford. It's just that he still carried an uneasy parsimonious air about him, but it was a denial not aimed toward himself or the things he provided for his family. Along with his lack of self-denial, there was also a Catholic sense of guilt for his materialistic behavior. He could not control it, he enjoyed it, and he did not want to sacrifice it and offer it up to God or to his fellow man. He was embarrassed about his success with false humility. He still wanted to make sure that you knew who he was and what he had managed to obtain for himself and for his family. He was proud of the success he felt he had achieved, like someone who liked to see if someone was looking at them with envy without their knowing it.

He micro-managed people but he did not realize he was doing it. He had a natural tendency for impatience and single-minded meanness, which affected his relationships with the people with whom he worked.

There was only one other person I had known who could match his temper and hot-headedness. He was a manager when Jon Serginalde, the regal old Swede was still the CEO. Back then, the state-of-the-art main frame computers used stacks of IBM cards for data input. There was a lot of manual effort before you got the computer printouts of the business results, and there was a lot of pressure when the books were closed and the reports were run.

This unfortunate manager frequently succumbed to the pressure and had a tendency to become overly excited and stressed. His outbursts could be heard from the front to the back of the office, and down the hall to the director's suite. Each time he had one of his disruptive outbursts he would be summoned to the director's office by the director's secretary. She wore very short, tight skirts, and if she was feeling sympathetic to all of us men, she would bend over and lean on a window sill to look out at the weather, and thus flash what little she was wearing underneath for us all to see. The anticipation of her sympathetic exhibitions took our minds off the overly stressed manager with a calming effect, and then she would lead him the down the hall to the director's office. The oldest, most experienced man in our office, a man who walked with difficulty because of a war injury to one of his hips, christened her, "thunder thighs." Not very original, but it was true.

She was always sweet to him and she did not mind.

In the old Swede's time, it was still a company where if you went to work and did your job each day, you could expect to have a job for life. It was not a place to get rich quick. It was intended that your personal wealth would grow with the slow and steady increase of the company's stock price. Savings would accumulate over time with the small and steady amounts that came out of your paycheck each month. You were expected to show up each day and get wealthy little by little over a long career. You owned the stock for the dividends as much or even more than for the stock price, because it was a GDP company, not a growth company, and you were not going to sell the stock, you were going to keep it to fund the purchase of a home and to make for a comfortable retirement. If you were at a high enough level, an executive level, ruthlessness, dispassion, and a lack of patience was deemed acceptable in order to get things done in the pitiless business world. If you were at that salary level it meant that your performance for the company was extremely valuable, your worth to the company was certified. It meant you performed your duties with intelligence, dedication, and hard work, and would get the job done with whatever it took.

I have never begrudged anyone who made their success to the highest levels, because they would almost always have to have earned it, and if not earned outright, to keep it meant continued successful effort or you were out. It was difficult, intelligent work. There may have been lifetime employment expectations for good performers at lower levels, but if you were a highly compensated executive, you performed or you were out, and there were no tears at your leaving. If you did not perform there were few second chances.

I learned later that the impatient, hot-headed manager was let go. His value to the company did not offset his behavioral shortcomings. But along with all the other young trainees with whom I started with the company, we were intimidated by the operational general managers and directors because of their aggressive lack of patience, coarse speech, and outbursts when unfavorable business results were communicated. Raised voices and colorful speech could be heard down the hall from their conference rooms. These men, and they were nearly all aggressive, unsmiling men, had value to the company that excused the limits of their behavior. They paid for it with performance. Too often it was accompanied by hard drinking, and family troubles, if the ability to cope with an aggressive business climate was not exceeded by the financial rewards it might have afforded to the executive and their family.

Later of course, a new chief executive changed all the promises of lifetime employment, and many other things at our slow and steady growth company. He accelerated a lot of things, but the brakes didn't work very well on some of the turns. The law of large numbers finally enforced itself in the marketplace. The speed, and some of the numbers generated by the speed with which we did business and closed deals, was not sustainable.

Anderson could be like a big teddy bear when things went well, especially after a business review where he had all the answers written down on hard copies of the presentations he would prepare. He tried to prepare for all the questions that might be asked. It was a good practice to follow, and he was especially pleased when there were no unanticipated questions which required follow-up. It irritated him if you could not answer a question during a review. It was unacceptable to him if we had to push the mute button on the speakerphone to discuss something quickly off-line, and then have to admit the lack of an answer back on-line.

"I'll have to get back to you for an answer on that," was not an answer he liked to use during a business discussion.

In the morning after a successful review, he liked to come down the hall from his staff office and chat with his managers for a few minutes, a cup of coffee or a diet cola in his hand. He would try to force a casual smile and stand in the doorway of one of our offices, and we'd come out into the hallway and talk. In this way he thought he validated his success with us. He really did attempt to be friendly, but he wasn't good at it. He still always seemed uncomfortable. He was a Midwest introverted transplant trying to force an extroversion with us born and bred southerners.

In response to his friendly gestures, we blocked the entrances to our offices by standing in the doorways as if we were glad to see him and had come out to talk. What we were really doing was standing in our doorways so that he could not walk in. If he did enter your office, he would stand next to your file cabinet and lean on it while he talked, picking up all the company memorabilia or product samples you collected over the years, to look at them and rearrange them. But as often as not, he liked to come behind your desk and lean over your shoulder because he enjoyed looking at what you were working on. This we all found was the singular most uncomfortably irritating experience of his management style. There was no escaping it, and over time we learned to grudgingly tolerate it. There was nothing we could do about it. It was just the way Troy acted. It was his nearly eccentric manner.

One day Troy came into my office in a particularly fine mood. He stood next to my file cabinet, and started picking up my product samples and putting them back down in different places, occasionally asking me to describe what they were and how they were used, what were their physical properties or cost, whether they were discontinued products, or test samples of new product introductions. He had already moved into a new home after successfully selling the house at the location from which he had come. It was a tremendous upgrade for him and his family, and he had earlier asked me my advice for the better neighborhoods in the suburbs where I lived. It was going to be a one way move for him, from the colder more expensive Midwest, to a less expensive warmer south. He anticipated a significantly lower cost of living, and he was going to make the most of it.

He would never go back to the Midwest he said, and he told me he had made a particularly good deal before he sold his old home. It had required an expensive foundation repair which he had to complete before he put it up for sale. A small local construction company had done the work, a family run business with a bookkeeper's wife, and a few long-term employees who had become like family over the years. It was the kind of business that would give you an honest quote, that was good with or without the paper it might be handwritten on. It was a more-than-one-generation small business that was honest and dependable, whose employees lived among the people for whom they performed their work.

His eyes lit up when he described his good fortune and astute business acumen, his careful handling of the repair contract he let out on his former property. The construction company had never sent him a bill for the work completed. At almost ten thousand dollars it was the most expensive maintenance he had ever had to incur on the old place. He had performed minimal maintenance on the home while he owned it, he could justify no major renovations if his family would not stay long enough to enjoy them. There was no sense in spending money to benefit the next owner of the house, even if he could get the money returned when it was sold. It was too much of a risk for his temperament and personality.

Troy took pride in the fact that even though he had set aside the money for the foundation repair, it had not yet been billed. He viewed it as a most improbable and fortuitous windfall. He had moved to a new home in a new city, and a bill had never been presented for the work done on his old home. He doubted that the contractor would ever discover the mistake. He believed that the contractor's wife would never discover the billing omission which was already more than a year in arrears. He was now living in another state in another part of the country. He left no forwarding address. It made him chuckle with the thought of the money which was still in his bank account where it would most likely remain, unclaimed by the company which had performed the foundation repair.

Now we needed to prepare for the next business review, and we had reminisced enough about the best personal business deal he had ever made. We needed to be meticulous in the preparation and documentation of the results of our business, so as not to cast aspersions on his ability to manage and control the business results. We all gathered as a team in the conference room to work together to footnote the schedules and charts he prepared. There would be no question on the integrity of our results and the explanations of our numbers that he would insist on presenting himself, personally, to higher management.

After all, we belonged to one of the world's truly great enterprises. Troy had a reputation to uphold, and we had our jobs to hold onto. Aside from that, there was no longer a guarantee, if there had ever really been one, of the security of lifetime employment, and the integrity and the judgement of our senior executives.

7.
Ash Wednesday

Shawn McGrath taught me what an invoice was, and just about everything else I needed to know in my first year at work. I did not want to admit that I did not know how to define what an invoice was from a technical accounting standpoint when I started my new job on the business management program. In my one and only business-related class I had taken at the university, introductory economics, we did not talk about such practical tools. I could graph a demand and supply curve, I knew how to use a slide rule because I took lots of science and math classes in high school and at the university, and I drew lots of graphs for chemistry and physics classes. I knew how to draw and explain organic chemical reactions and how the symbols for the compounds changed step by step in the reactions, but the technical definition of an invoice was beyond me, and I could not disguise this fact. I suddenly realized that the laws of nature did not apply here and I soon learned that nobody in the accounting department cared if I knew how to diagram an organic chemical reaction. But they did notice what kind of shoes I wore and my shoes did not measure up. Unfortunately, this was before western boots were stylish accessories and they simply called me cowboy because I grew up in the Midwest, as if it were a foreign country beyond the other side of the state. I was a Midwest Protestant working in a predominantly Catholic northeast city, and I had not yet earned enough to buy a new set of clothes and business shoes.

It was critical for me to understand what an invoice was because in my first job it was my responsibility to recommend when we issued credits against invoices for claims made by our customers. I found myself in Customer Accounting, whatever that was, and at first the name made no sense to me. You know you are further and further down the wrong path when names no longer make sense. "Claims and Credits Department" even I could have understood. It took me a while to understand that in this office, Customer Accounting meant a very specific function. And a simple example would explain it.

If a truck which was delivering one of our very large pieces of equipment hit a highway overpass because the truck was loaded too high, it was my job to determine how the claim should be settled for the loss that occurred. Shawn explained interesting situations where highly skilled and experienced truck drivers knew the exact height of their loads, and the exact clearance of a particular overpass, and if there was a dip in the road under the overpass. If the driver was good enough, he could sense how fast he needed to approach the dip in the road, to compress the springs of the truck trailer enough at the bottom of the dip so that the load would pass under the bridge without a catastrophic collision.

He told me this so convincingly that I actually believed him. I did not recognize the disgust in his eyes when he realized my naivete.

Still, it was a very useful introduction for me to the business world, where terms and conditions were the basis of promises made, and problematic outcomes were evaluated. It was a world with mostly gray conclusions, and more rarely black and white results, the kind of results I had learned to understand with the natural reactions of chemistry and physics, that did not apply in business.

I thought this particular example was an expensive game to play with trucks and loads and bridges, but I could not tell if Shawn was making fun of me or telling the truth and I thought I needed to play it safe and listen to him. He was testing me to see how hard or soft boiled I was, how intelligent, how nasty, whether I was too cocksure, or perhaps even worse, how naive.

He made fun of me because I was from the Midwest and he was from the east coast, and that made him clearly superior. He had seen too many trainees like me come and go. After a while, after they started calling me cowboy, and talked about me being from out west even though it was only one state away, he discovered that I actually knew how to spell and read and do simple math equations. I had come from a Midwestern land grant school and at first, he had not been certain. After a while he began to see that I paid attention to the things he tried to teach me, and that I did understand how to add and subtract, multiply and divide.

The secretary in our department, she called him, "Shawnie." He was liked by all of the secretaries, especially the younger ones. He was the oldest man in our office and knew everything about it, and had seen everything through the years, and the secretaries knew he would make no unreasonable demands on them. Patti was particularly fond of Shawn, and although she was from another department, he understood her and would kindly call her his pet. He always told her to behave herself and clucked his tongue at her with disapproval when he thought the clothes she wore were too revealing, and displayed too much of her charm.

Patti worked for one of the younger managers who had a different name for her than the one Shawn used, when she wore her short skirts and colorful underclothes. She knew about the names, and knew that there was much to like about Shawn, even though he was certainly old enough to be her father. He had a huge powerful looking, square shaped head, he still had most of his hair, and his face looked like he could have been a boxer when he was young or in the service. It was said he injured one of his hips in WWII, somewhere in Italy, and it caused him to walk with a pronounced limp. He wouldn't talk about it. If you looked at him, his face reminded you of a bloodhound. The skin hung in folds around his eyes, and nose, and mouth, but he still retained a masculine handsomeness. It sometimes made him look weary, especially when his patience was being tested by the trainees who did not know anything at the start of their careers. He was very smart about the work, and he was street smart, too. He grew up in some rowhouse neighborhood, and at one time or another he was hung out of a window by his feet between classes by the hoodlums at the catholic school he attended because he was short and did not know how to keep his mouth shut. By the time he grew up, you could imagine he might have done the same thing to one or two of the younger students at the school who crossed him the wrong way. Big city Catholic schoolroom violence seemed to be a rite of passage in parts of this city. He told me that the Nuns would break rulers over your knuckles over the slightest infraction, and if you really made them angry, you'd get the splinters shoved into your hands as well. Shawn said that a nun's level of sexual frustration determined the extent of their physical abuse against the boys in the school, especially for the most handsome ones, such as he described himself.

If Shawn had to explain something to you more than once, he would look at you with his tired drooping eyes, as if you were the most thick-headed person in the world, and why were you wasting his time? What was your problem that you did not understand? He did not want you to know if he liked you, and he treated those he liked the same way as with those whom he did not like, with practiced indifference. With irritated indifference is how he treated me and the other young female trainee with whom I worked together with Shawn. I loved that girl, but she was already married. Unfortunately, her husband was in law enforcement, taller than me, better looking, and outweighed me by at least thirty pounds.

Personal computers had not yet been invented, and our mainframe computer ran the reports for our general ledger. We all used electronic calculators, while some of the older guys used calculators that also had a paper roll, so that you could print out a set of numbers for a receipt of your work. None of the young trainees used paper roll calculators. It reminded me of the kinds of receipts you got at the grocery store. Even my high school girlfriend could produce a receipt when she sold me cigarettes at the corner store when I was too young to buy them for myself. Shawn, on the other hand, did not use a modern desk top calculator of any kind. He used a machine I had never seen before. He worked it with both hands, and used multiple fingers of each hand, and it required the user to pull on a mechanical arm to complete the mechanical transaction. He could add, subtract, multiply, and divide with it. I had never before seen a Comptometer.

Shawn was still using a mechanical model WM Comptometer, not a more modern electric Comptometer model. The electric version was the pinnacle of the line, manufactured several years after the mechanical marvel he still used was manufactured. You need to understand that this is a machine that was invented in the nineteenth century. Still, he was able to calculate numbers faster with that old machine than the new trainees were able to do at first with their modern electronic machines. He rarely made a mistake and worked multiple keys with as many fingers as it took to enter a number of any size. This was a machine that had been made more than thirty years earlier, when Shawn was still fighting the Fascists in Italy. It was made out of steel and aluminum, not plastic, and contained no silicone chips. When his Comptometer was made, silicone chips had not yet been invented. Eventually, an electric version of the comptometer would be produced, but it too had been discontinued many years before.

He insisted it gave him a feel for the numbers, using this old outdated technology that had been invented almost a hundred years earlier. Over time I also grew to know what it was to get a feel for the numbers, and though I never used a Comptometer, it did not matter what the latest technology was as long as you "touched" the numbers yourself, as Shawn would say. In some intangible way you needed to develop a feel for the numbers that enabled you to let them speak.

There was one thing Shawn did teach me that I have never forgotten. It was a lesson I did not understand at the time, and a lesson he never explained to me. I know now that he was able to recognize, what I did not yet know and understand. My lack of living and experience would later become for me, a recognition of different cultures and sensibilities, and an ability to hold back judgement, and to have enough confidence to remain silent. He took a kind of pity on me for not knowing certain things and for my lack of experience of life in the east, or anywhere else other than where I had come from. It meant that he did not want to explain it to me and expose my ignorance in the office. He knew I would eventually learn these things, and it seemed to me much later that he was in fact not at all consumed by the east coast pride and egoistic self-importance that I had originally attributed to him. He was from the city. That was all that mattered to him. I recognize now that it was kind of him not to do what he could have done, and expose me to the ridicule of the colleagues in our office. I was still months away from my first-year anniversary with the company. When you are in business it takes at least a year to experience the annual cycles and seasonal activities of the market. For other things, I would come to learn that it takes a lifetime to try to understand.

It happened on a Wednesday, the 12th of February. I had finally begun to feel a bit more confident when I got to the office each day to do my job. I rarely beat Shawn to the office, and it was on a day when for some reason he was late. I had been working for a while when he finally came in. When I saw him, I figured he had brushed up against something in the city on the way to work, or in the parking lot when he got out of his car. The city could really be a dirty, gritty place, as was the employee parking lot around our old multi-story factory. An acid pickling bath for cleaning steel parts was located right beside the parking lot. By the end of my first year of parking there, the fumes had already taken the paint off the top of my car. I thought I was doing him a favor when I noticed the dirt on his forehead, and I told him about it so that he could wipe it off, feeling an equality and a collegial recompense, for all he had done to help me.

Shawn McGrath, in his kindness and without repudiation, grunted and said nothing back to me, sat down at his desk and got on with his work. He dismissed me quietly without anyone else hearing, and no one else would know what this young, midwest Protestant said to the older, big city Catholic, on the morning of my first Ash Wednesday in the office of the city.

8.
A Walk at Mepkin

The Abbot Father had already played the organ and said Mass in the Mepkin Chapel for the last time. Now, he could no longer walk, was on oxygen and morphine, and he was confined to a wheelchair. His family spent his last week together with him, and they had time to say their goodbyes. The simple funeral arrangements would be carried out based on the Order of the Cistercians, Mass and burial with attendance for family and the brothers of the monastery only. A memorial service later would be open to the public.

In his last month, the Mepkin Abbey web site informed the public that with his illness, the Abbot's time was measured in days and weeks, no longer weeks and months. It was to be a grace-filled time in the midst of a grieving monastic community. It was a decreasing, a dying, the slow diminishment of a brother called The Abbot.

At 6:47pm I received a telephone call to inform me that he had passed away. A younger brother was with the Abbot when he died, along with all the brothers of Mepkin. The web site said later that he died at 5:35pm on Sunday, August 27, 2006. He was 57 years old.

The Drive South

The funeral was held at 10am Wednesday August 30 at the church of Mepkin Abbey. Only the monastic community and the family were in attendance. A public Memorial Service was scheduled for Thursday, August 31 at 5pm in the Luce Gardens of Mepkin Abbey, Moncks Corner, near Charlestown, South Carolina.

I drove south on Wednesday, intending to drive as far as I was able to, and arrive to the Abbey on Thursday. But by the end of the day of the funeral, the memorial service scheduled for Thursday was delayed until Friday. The inclement weather of Hurricane Ernesto made an angry landfall in South Carolina at the end of the funeral service, and the storm raged for a day.

On Friday afternoon I crossed the Wadboo Bridge and drove the final six miles on Dr. Evans Road to Mepkin Abbey. Dr. Evans Road takes you past an incongruous assortment of old farm places, fundamental Christian churches, pockets of suburban developments, horse and cattle pastures, and an occasional plantation property. The closer to the Abbey, the more bucolic the setting, until you arrive at the entrance gates, and meet, at St. Peter's guest house, the majestic drive of the Abbey lined with ancient live oaks draped with the filigree of Spanish moss.

At the reception center and gift shop, I was greeted by a man and woman who informed me that I could see the gardens if I wanted to. When I told them that I wanted to attend the memorial service, they said it was scheduled at 5pm, and that I could walk in the gardens until then. They asked where I was from and I quietly told them.

It was already two days since the Abbot, the son, brother, cousin, friend, was buried. He had been carried from the church on an open bier, wearing only a monk's cowl. A shroud was placed to cover his face before he was lowered into the earth. Each of the family members and religious in turn took a handful of soil and let it fall onto the shroud and cowl of the Abbot, before the grave was filled up and the earth was packed against him.

The Memorial Service

On Friday afternoon, volunteers directed cars to parking places and showed the memorial guests the way to the Luce gardens which were positioned on a high bluff overlooking a grand bend of the Cooper River. Three thousand chairs had been set up that morning in the sun of the hot, humid morning that became the day, adding to the fatigue that had drained one's strength from the events of the week.

The seats in front of the stage faced away from the river bluff, but directly into the sun. In the front row to the side of the stage an overhang of a live oak created the only area of protective shade. Chamber musicians began to arrange their places on stage, but because of the strength of the sun, it was decided that they would move off the stage, to the right side by the edge of the river bluff. The chairs for the speakers were rearranged to put the sun at their sides in the very hot and humid late afternoon.

People began to arrive, and those who had personally known the Abbot greeted his parents with warmth and humility, thanking them for their son, and what he had done not only for the Church and the community, but for their own personal lives. One man, who would later speak to the audience from the stage, told his parents that the friendship offered him by their son had changed his life, and the Governor held both of their hands as he said this, struggling to keep his composure as he spoke.

Friends of the dead Abbot who spoke at the memorial expressed their respect and love to the mother and father, and for all of the brothers as well. The prior of the Abbey, the pastor of St. Johannes Lutheran, the vicar of St. James Episcopal, and the General Superior of the Sisters of Charity of Our Lady of Mercy, who had helped tend to the Abbot during his treatments at Sloan Kettering in New York City. The Governor of South Carolina, the Director of Charleston Cultural Affairs, the President and Chairman of the Center for Humans and Nature, and the Abbot of Guadalupe Abbey and President of the U.S. Region, who was an intimate friend of the Abbot during the years he spent in Europe, all spoke. All of these and many others embraced the family and the monastic community, offering condolences and thanks for the life of the beloved Abbot.

In the distance, alone with a few family members beneath the shade of a separate live oak draped with Spanish moss, sat the former U.S. Senator from South Carolina, who was quoted in the Charleston Post and Courier.

"If ever there was a saint, he was one…," said the former Senator of his friend, the Abbot of Mepkin Abbey.

The Abbot was a cloistered monk who gave himself up to God, had given himself also to his friends and the larger community and to the world outside of the monastery when it was required. He was a reluctant participant in worldly affairs, but one who could disarm a banker or a politician alike with the threat of a higher authority and a well-chosen word. The shoes he wore were old and worn out, because he gave away the new ones his mother sent him, to anyone who needed them more than him. He knew how to bring people together, how to appeal to the best of what we are, how to laugh and love and weep, and how to appreciate and live a life of beauty and the arts, with contemplation and devotion to the works of the Church.

"He was our own St. Francis," the Governor said during his remarks that afternoon.

The Memorial concluded with a final word from the Abbot himself, written to his closest friends and colleagues in the Trappist community thirteen days before he died, knowing that the end was near.

"I am now with God. He is my only option," he began.

And with a final admonishment to all of us with respect to surrendering our own lives.

"It is later than you think."

The Service ended with the chamber musicians and the hymn, "Brother James' Air" (Psalm 23).

After the service I went over to where the musicians had been playing and looked out over the bend of the Cooper River, a hundred feet below the cliff and stretching a half mile to the other side. A young reporter from the Post and Courier stood talking to the family. He did not know the Abbot well, but had met him four times. The family told him that when he was growing up, he was ashamed that he was not athletic like his father who had been a champion athlete. The Abbot was a classically trained professional musician who played the organ and piano before he became a priest. But his father said he always told him, that he was prouder of him than he could ever have been, for any sport that he might have played.

The Abbot was a graduate of the Julliard School, a concert organist who played the complete works of Bach in weekly concerts from memory, once in New York City, and once in Philadelphia. All this before he became a priest, a Trappist Monk, an Abbot first at the Abbey of Gethsemani in Trappist, Kentucky, and finally the Abbot at Mepkin Abbey, at Moncks Corner, South Carolina.

I walked the grounds of Mepkin with his mother while the rest of the family returned to St. Peter House. We went first to the terraces of the Luce Gardens which led down to the river below where the memorial took place and where the Luce family cemetery was, then past the lake where alligators swam, and across the gardens to the Abbey buildings. Here was the new church that the Abbot built, the new refectory, the library, and the new infirmary, and I passed the low building which housed the grand piano purchased by the Abbey with the help of a thankful benefactor, the instrument on which he practiced. We made our way to his grave in the garden outside of the church, in the middle of the burying ground overlooking the Cooper River.

Shuddering with tears, I held her.

"A parent is not supposed to bury a child," wept his grieving mother.

We left, and passed through the church again, and entered the guest refectory, separated by a glass partition from where the brothers ate their meals. The head table on the other side of the partition was where the Abbot would sit, with the Prior at his side, in front of the two rows of tables where the monks ate in silence.

A man was eating in the guest refectory, a simple vegetable soup and coarse bread. He had known the Abbot well, he said, the general contractor for the Abbey's building programs.

It was now seven o'clock.

The Compline

We returned to the church for the Compline, the last service of the day before the monks retired to their individual cells, a celebration of the day with twenty minutes of songs and prayers. There were five retreatant guests also in the church. We all sat on the right side in partitioned oak pews with folding seats. A friend of Mepkin who visited often and had known the Abbot for twelve years, sat with us to my left, with his mother and his father to my right.

The simple service began with the ringing of the bells and a knock at the door. The Prior entered to lead the singing, bowing deeply, and singing to each side of the church in turn from the other. We and the brothers ended this day as they do each day, in evensongs of prayer. The prior received the holy water as the service ended, and the brothers of the Abbey and the guests all walked to the front of the church from each side of the pews, then turning to the middle of the church we filed in a single row to the alter, where we each bowed and received the asperges, the rite of sprinkling with holy water, from the Prior.

Exiting the doors to the left of the church we entered into the garden. I walked over to stand with the Abbot's mother who was already by the fresh grave, looking down at the place where her son should not be. I put my arm around her and held her hands as she wept and put her face against my shoulder.

The Return

In a few minutes we were back at St. Peter house and I took my leave. In this evening my place was at a hotel in Moncks Corner. The family would return to their homes the next day.

I left the driveway and drove back to town.

The six miles of Doc Evans Road brings you back to the present from the place where time slows down among the mossy oaks, the Spanish moss, and the gardens of Mepkin Abbey; and the banks of the Cooper River and the water that flows through it. By the time you cross Wadboo Bridge you have returned back to the world, and lost the dream of all that happened that week. And the final day at Mepkin Abbey is gone.

9.
Surrender

Nik warned her about soldiers and sailors, and the boys back home.

"Don't surrender yourself to this guy," he wrote to her before he sailed on the LST to the Solomon Islands Campaign at Bougainville.

"And by the way, you are now elected the company pinup girl. Your picture made a hit with 'We the Marines!' Don here, who is just a typical marine in uniform as well as out, calls you Curvaceous, and sends a request for a picture of you in a sweater. He says you are letting a lot of curves go to waste by not wearing one…"

Your friend, Nik

"I was a little surprised when I received your letter today. I had a swell time talking to you and your friend, and when we said goodbye at the station, I thought you would write, but not so soon. It was a swell trip when you went along. After you left the train, things got rather dull."

Hope to see you again, Ray

"Tonight, it's raining cats and dogs, and though I'm in a tent it is a very leaky one, and I can't seem to keep dry. A tent can only last so long against so much rain, you know. By the way, your letter took eleven days to get here, so I'm not doing so bad either, am I?"

"Boy, your family really has scattered, no? When does Rudi ship out? I hope he gets his furlough. Has he been to L.A. or Hollywood? Tell him to go to the Hollywood Canteen and meet some of the stars. It will be very crowded but they are swell people to meet. Tell him also to go to the Palladium if he gets a chance. They have swell bands there, and it is one of the most modern dance halls in the US."

As ever, Nik

"I am reading between the lines, but I believe you are a little interested. Do you want to know what I think of you? I think you are nice all the way around. But I lied a little about myself. If I thought you were just another girl, I would let things go as they are but I think too much of you already. The soldier with me was not my brother, he got on the train with me in Toledo. I do have two brothers though, one is eighteen and is in the South Pacific, and the other fourteen still at home. I do not have a sister. I have lived in Toledo for the past ten years."

"I am a submarine sailor, twenty-three years old, in the service two years, and at sea training for more than a year now. I regret feeding you a line like I did on the train. After you left, I got to thinking a little and I know now that you could mean too much to me to lie to you."

Hope to see you soon, Ray

"But seriously, Katarine, I think you did what was right, for you should know if you care for a fellow or not, and how much. He probably didn't like it at all, you not letting him kiss you, for if a fellow likes a girl really well, he surely wants to kiss her. A fellow will admire a girl a lot more if she doesn't go in for necking too much, at least I do. Of course, there are fellows who don't. If one really likes the other a lot, then it's only human that they should."

"Wait! What am I getting into? I don't like to give lectures and this isn't one either, just a friendly letter to one of my best friends. I don't mind you telling me at all, Katarine. In fact, I like to know about you and what is going on back there. Thanks, dear, for wishing me back home soon. I too wish I could get there as soon as possible. I'd sure like to go bicycle riding with you, but I don't know about hiking, for I've done too much of that already. Send me a picture of you in your bicycle uniform, you know, the shorts and sweater outfit? Darn, why is the film so hard to get? I enclose a note asking you to get film for me, but keep it for your camera. I guess it's easier if you have a request from a soldier."

Your friend, Nik

"I have been to many places and met a lot of girls. But the girls at sea ports and large cities are no match for the girls back home. None can compare and you don't realize how fortunate you are to live inland, and I hope things can develop between us."

"I want to find out if you will leave me. Our letters will decide if we ever see each other again. There is something about you I love and it would be nice to have someone to come home to."

"About my girlfriend. After not being home to make things interesting for her she found someone else and married him! Now I want someone who is not afraid and will wait for me. I hope it might be you. I will be careful, please do the same and take care of yourself. I am going to mail this in Philadelphia on my way to the port in Connecticut. But the next letter will probably go through the censors. When I come back again, I hope you will be near."

I hope to hear from you soon, Ray

"I guess you are wondering what has become of me. No, it isn't that I have forgotten, not after growing up with you and knowing you for so long. A lot has happened since I last wrote you, and you have probably read about it. But first of all, I want to thank you loads for the swell package you sent me. I really enjoyed it. Even more because it was from an old friend, and I am chewing the gum you enclosed with the other things faster than I can write this letter."

"I was at the campaign at Bougainville, and really kept quite busy for almost two months. We were the first Marines to land under fire and I sure was glad our boat got safely to shore. But after we did get to shore, we kept busy dodging the bullets from the sky when a Nips would break away from an American plane. I saw plenty of air and naval battles on the first few days. Then came our task of pushing inland and we were mostly on our own then."

"We were in the major battle of 'Hand Grenade Hill,' named so because of the many grenades we got thrown at us when we tried to take the hill. We were on the front lines for fifty-seven days and it rained almost every day."

"There is an active volcano on the isle and also a few earthquakes here. It's funny, it is really very beautiful on a clear day, but I'd rather see it in a picture."

Your friend, Nik

"Dear, here I am in New London, Connecticut. The weather is nice and cool. I suppose you want to know how I feel. Well, I lost about ten pounds on this last trip, but I feel good now that I can get some rest."

"I am leaving again soon. So, I probably won't be around for Christmas. I got three letters and a box from you yesterday. Thanks a lot, darling. I really appreciate the box and letters."

All my love, Ray

"Dear Swiss Miss, it's true that the native girls here are very pretty, and they look just like they do in the movies, but their personalities are bunk. Dorothy Lamour would look like one of them in her slippers and a short dress, because they don't wear sarongs here. But they do wear flowers in their hair, and they like to look white and they wear big sun hats to keep the tan off their faces. Some of them are whiter than me with my dark tan.

And they are very shy until you get to know them, and then they always want to see you. I have to be good, Katarine, for we get no liberty here. It's been fifteen months since I've had any, and the only time I get to meet the lovely native girls is when I'm on guard duty and they come walking down the street. So, I've met Dolores, Rosettea, Moano, and Mary, who is a widow. The Japs killed her husband and cut off all her hair. She wears a scarf on her head all the time, and she looks very pretty as long as she keeps her scarf on. They also have a very funny accent to their English, for most are of Spanish descent."

"But Swiss Miss, this is not what I wanted to talk about, and I sure wish I could be having a conversation with you instead, and we could be going on that dancing date of ours at the Moonlight Ballroom, but I'm in my tent, on my cot, writing you this letter by candlelight. I've got to go now, Swiss Miss, for they're shooting dice right at the foot of my bunk and the language they're using isn't fit to be heard while I am writing to you, dear."

Love & Kisses, Nik – "Mind?"

"This letter is going to be short but sweet, I hope. I will write a longer one when I get back to the rest camp. I can't think of the questions you asked and will have to go back and get them and read them again."

"I can't think straight now. I am so worn out it is hard to sit down and write. I hope you will excuse the way this is written. I think of you every day, wondering what you are doing and if you love me. Here is all my love. Now I can go to bed and dream."

All my love, Ray

"Dearest Swiss Miss, forgive me for not writing, dear, but I had to go through another campaign and I am sure that your prayers did help, for this one was plenty rough, and I was plenty scared several times. It was the Mariana Islands Campaign, which you probably heard of and read about. Please excuse this V-mail but it is all I can get a hold of right now, and as soon as I can I shall write you a long letter. I'll ask you for one film for my camera then you keep it, take the pictures, and send me a few. I hear they are easier to get that way. So, bye for now and I'll try not to let 'em get me down, even though it was pretty hard at times."

Love, Nik

"Do you think it's possible for me to fall in love with you through letters and only seeing you once? You don't hear from me very often, but you are always on my mind and heart. I often wonder who is taking you to the show that night, while I am in my bunk on the sub, or if you went skating. I wonder if he is the high school boy next door who is always trying to kiss you, or if it is your boss. I guess I think of a million things like that. Then I wonder how it would be if I were there to share such things with you."

"When you left me on the train and got off, I wanted to kiss you. I tried to make it sound like a joke when I asked you. But I really meant it. Maybe I shouldn't have asked you because I figured you thought I was trying to be fresh. But now I wish I could have kissed you. I would have it as a reminder that there is someone who might love me."

All my love, Ray

"My dear Swiss Miss, yes, I am fine, thanks, and feel well too, after receiving your letter. I am now writing this inside a pup tent and for light I have a candle. I guess I am sort of fortunate in having one. We are kept quite busy out here and this is the only time I have to drop you a line. How soon I can mail it, I don't know, mail doesn't go out here regular right now. All the fellows are gathered around a fire they built and talking of home or what they should do on their furlough. I'd rather be here writing to you, mind? I like to think of the swell times our families had together."

Love & Kisses, Nik

"I know I have only been with you once but there was something about you which attracted me and your letters mean a lot me. Your letter was just like a fellow wants them. If I am cutting in on anyone's territory, please let me know. I don't want to make a fool of myself."

"I did receive your picture and it looks nice hanging on my locker door. The fellows with me wonder how I can be so sure about a girl I have seen only once. They say I am in love with a memory and a picture. What do you think? I suppose a civilian has snowed you under which lets a submarine sailor out in the wind since in this time I got no more mail from you."

"Oh yes, I got busy and studied, and I made 2/class."

Love, Ray

"Know what, dear? We finally got a radio and they rebroadcast it from here on the island. I heard the three songs you told me about, and I think I like, "Dance with the Dolly with the Hole in her Stocking," the best. They are all swell though. I also heard Frankie sing, and say – he isn't bad – what do you think? Now that we do have something nice, we will probably move out, for as soon as things get a little comfy, the Marines pull out, you can bet on it! I don't think we'll go on any pleasure cruise, either."

"Toad sent me a picture, he sure looks swell and big. He is now 6 ft and weighs 190 lbs. I still am only 5'7" and weigh 175 lbs. My little brother really outgrew me."

"Boy, your brothers are really spread out, your family is really doing their part in the war. Gosh, Tom really saw the Buzz bombs in London? He shall have a lot to tell. What is he doing in France? So, you think Jimmy is now in France in combat? I sure hope he comes through it."

"I sure do remember the swell New Year's parties we used to have, Katarine, and hope everyone shall be there soon to enjoy them again. Bye for now and I hope you have luck in getting some film, for I love to receive snaps from you."

"Well Dear, adios, and be good."

Love, Nik

"You wanted to know about my work, well there is not much to tell. This trip has been a good one. Everything ran well, no breakdowns or anything. I am getting very white, I look pale. We see the sun once in a while, but not recently. The submarine is like a city. It has its own power plant, phone system, etc. I work on all of the electrical equipment, in fact almost everything on a sub runs by electric."

"The next letter from me will probably be from another city. Sorry, but I can't say what city."

My love, Ray

"Dearest Katarine, I have just received a swell valentine from you. I really appreciate it very much. It indeed means a lot to me, it was swell of you to think of me and coming from you, Swiss Miss. I look forward to every one of your letters very much and you can imagine I also look forward to seeing you!"

"Yesterday I saw my second white woman in twenty-one months over here. They were Navy nurses and whisked by us in a station wagon. We were just coming back from a ten-mile hike. As for morale, they are no good. Your letters help much more, Swiss Miss."

Love, Nik

"It doesn't look like I will get home for some time. Now I am in California and expect to leave here before long to go to the war zone in the Pacific to relieve someone. If you ever find someone, don't be afraid to tell me. If you ever think it best for me to forget you, please let me know. I will try to understand. I am not much good at writing letters, but I hope you can see what I am trying to say."

"I have loved you ever since I met you. But my luck has been bad. It has been a long time since I saw you. If I ever get back home and can see you again, and you are still single, I will want to take you with me."

Love, Ray

"Dear Swiss Miss, I was very shocked to hear that Jimmy is missing-in-action. I hope it is only a mistake and that you'll find out about it soon. It often happens over here, when they get lost from one outfit and go with another. The news really hurt and I hope and pray that he is safe. Let me know as soon as you hear any word from Jimmy. Be with your mother as much as you can, for she needs her rest and sleep."

"You're swell dear, for not minding about my question about the sailor. I hope I see you soon, too, it's been well over two years now. I'm writing this aboard ship so after this I hope I get a chance to come home. Some of the fellows left for home already who came over with me, and a lot of fellows also went home through the hospital."

"Bye now dear, and write when you can."

Love, Nik

WAR & NAVY DEPARTMENTS
V-MAIL SERVICE
USMC REPORTS UNDELIVERABLE
RETURNED TO SENDER

February 26, 1945

"Dear Nik, Hi! And how are you? Fine and dandy, I hope. Got your letter today of no date, but it was a V-mail and I was glad to hear from you. Yes, Nik, I hope you can come home soon. I hope this war will end very soon, also."

"I know you are very 'busy' again Nik, but I hope and pray you will come through safely. I know what it is to have someone who is in battle, and I know how your family must feel. My sister-in-law is as good as can be expected since my brother Jimmy is still MIA."

"So, you don't feel that the nurses are 'morale' boosters? Tsk! Tsk! and I was thinking of joining the 'Cadet Nurses Corps.' Twenty-one months is a long time. It isn't fair to you boys to have to stay so long from home and life."

"Pardon this V-mail Nik, but I am out of air-mails. I will write you when I get some, OK? Take care of yourself, Nik."

"Adios, and God Bless You, 'cause we want you home."

Love, Katarine

Nik landed on the beach with the 3rd Marine Division on 24 February 1945 with the 1st Battalion, Company B, of the 9th Marines. The task for the veteran marines of this division was to secure the central portion of the island's northern plateau, and to attack down the ridges leading to the sea. On the second day, 25 February, the 9th Marines passed through the lines of the 21st Marines to attack Japanese Lieutenant General Tadamichi Kuribayashi's main island defenses.

The 1st and 2nd Battalions of the 9th waited together for the battle to begin, the 1st on the right and the 2nd on the left, beyond the front lines of the 21st Marines. Heavy U.S. artillery and naval gunfire prepared the killing fields and hillsides for the Marine's attack which began at 09:30. They would advance upon the commanding ground of Hill 200-P from which the Japanese defended the Airfield Number 2.

There would be no surrender of any Japanese soldiers that day. And not even on the final day of the battle for the small Pacific Island, though it could not yet be known. On that final day, the Japanese would charge to fight in the open with their remaining exhausted, hungry, and thirsty forces, as if they wanted the killing of themselves to be finished and gotten over with quickly. But the killing on this day would not be quick, nor would it be easy, in the battle for Airfield Number 2. There would be no surrender this day.

All along the front, heavy small arms gunfire met each attempt of the Marines to advance, as the enemy defended their positions from well-concealed emplacements. Where the Battalions were shielded from one enemy position, they were exposed to raking fire from another, and enemy mortar, artillery, and rocket fire sighted in on each of their attempts to approach. The movement of battle stopped, started, and stopped and started again and again, each time with severe damage and cost of casualties to the 9th Marines exposed to the withering enemy fire.

The 1st Battalion crossed the E-W runway shielded by accompanying Sherman tanks, but anti-tank fire limited the effort. Tracers streaked by in both directions while the Marines followed closely behind the tanks, trying to shield themselves while mortars and artillery shells exploded against the four-inch-thick armor of the Sherman's, but did not stop their advance.

The Corporal would not see his Company B of the 1st Battalion advance to cross the NE-SW runway in the direction of Hill 200-P. The tank which he followed had tried to move up onto the runway and exposed its less armored underside to a mine. The explosion set off the ammunition inside the tank, thousands of rounds of .30 caliber machine gun ammo, hand grenades, and the high-explosive 75mm tank gun shells. From his position, Nik could not see and would not hear the called in artillery and naval gunfire support, nor see his buddies cross the second runway to gain a foothold at the base of Hill 200-P.

Nik now lay beside the sheltering tank, its hatches blown open and the turret thrown completely off, the five-man crew obliterated, then incinerated, its tracks run off and its empty hull stopped in the middle of the commanding ground of the Hill 200-P sector beside the NE-SW runway.

Machine gun fire had already dropped him before the tank blew and as he fell, he had watched his Marine buddy Don reach the edge of the airfield. For a moment he thought of his childhood friend Katarine, whom Don had named the Company B's pinup girl, "Curvaceous." Helpless, he felt something like fire move inside him and then through him.

"Now I'll be able to go back home and dance with Katarine," he thought as he lost consciousness, before the shrapnel of the tank explosion finished him off and killed him.

The battle would last for three more days before the 9th Marines controlled the two hills north of Airfield Number 2. Nik was one of five thousand nine hundred thirty-one Marines killed, and seventeen thousand three hundred seventy-two wounded, in the taking of the tiny Pacific atoll, Iwo Jima.

Sub Div 32, Guam

"I believe all of your letters have reached me now. I have been moved around so much it has taken a lot of time for my mail to catch up with me."

"You say a girl is supposed to keep a fellow guessing. You sure do. I try to read in-between the lines but I still can't figure you out. Once in a while you drop a hint on what is in your mind. I don't want to jump to conclusions and then be disappointed in the end. So, I will just have to take a chance, and hope you will be there when I get back."

"I hope I can get a few days rest now. I have a tough job on the ship I work on and am plenty tired. This heat takes all the pep out of me. What I wouldn't give for that Atlantic duty I had! It at least wasn't so hot. It was good duty compared to this."

"It is time for some sleep, so good night. Do you ever dream?"

All my love, Ray

Guam, Oct 3, 1945

"My Dear Miss Katarine,"

"I guess you will be rather surprised to hear from a person you have never seen. I am sorry that my letter has to be of such a sad nature."

"I found your September 24 letter to Ray today and enclose it in return. Being his best friend, we had a sort of friendship pact. This pact provided that if anything should happen to either one of us, the other would answer his mail and explain to all parties concerned."

"Ray started out on a run just before the war ended. We were sent out with Division 32 and he caught the run. A message was sent from his boat only about ten or twelve hours before the news came that Japan had surrendered, and up to now we are still waiting and hoping they will return. A motto of Ray's was 'Never Say Die,' but they are several weeks overdue and their loss seems positive."

"I guess you two thought quite a lot of each other. Ray spoke of you even more than I spoke of my own girlfriend. And to do that he had to talk all the time. But in my short span of life never have I met a person that I liked any more than I did him. Being the only son of a rather doting set of parents I never knew how it felt to know a brother's love, but Ray was my brother, even if it was by proxy. Possibly you think that after losing such a good friend my letter to you is not sorrowful enough. But he asked me that in case it was him who got it first, not to waste any sorrow on him."

"I am sending your letter back, but if I hear anything, I will keep your address so that I can write you."

"Please accept my regrets and deepest sympathy, but please share my hope he is ok."

Yours very truly,

Billy Jack Simmons, S 1/c (RM), Sub Div 32

September 24, 1945

"Dear Ray,"

"Hello, it's me again! I can't believe it's almost the end of September! You know it's been a long time since I've seen you. What have you been doing, as if I don't know? Still working you hard? Is there any chance of you coming home soon?"

"We folks here in the States hear such rumors as the boys who have been overseas two years or more will be sent back to the States. Is that true, or don't you men hear much about it? I'm asking a lot of questions in these two paragraphs, aren't I? But here's hoping you can come back soon."

"I am still working five days a week, and a Saturday every other weekend. How long I will continue to work here I can't say because I believe the boss is having a hard time keeping me. We have two soldiers working here now. One was a pilot and the other one I don't know as he just started yesterday. There are only two girls working here now including me. One is classified as a Clerk and I'm listed as a Lab Assistant. Someone thinks that I should be a Clerk. I am doing a little bit of everything now but still am listed as a Lab Assistant. So, you see, I don't know how long I'll work here. Sounds all mixed up, doesn't it? Someone is doing work now they don't like and maybe that is the reason, anyway no one else says anything. I am doing the best work I can, that's all that matters."

"Do you know sometimes I feel like going to a different city to start all over again? We all have had that feeling more than once, I suppose."

"Don't mind me, Ray."

"Do you like operas? I have never seen one, and 'Rigoletto' is coming here in October, so maybe I'll see it. Jean Dickenson stars in it. Have you ever heard her sing? She is very good."

"Where would you like to live, Ray? You have been to so many places now, maybe you have an idea of where you would like to live. Me, I love the Ohio scenery, but I'd like to go to some state where the climate is more pure and healthful, and of course that would probably mean the West."

"This morning was beautiful. The moon was shining in my window early this morning. These big full moons! I haven't been out looking at the moon with someone for a long time, Ray, besides my girlfriends. We just look at it, and turn away, and think...someday."

"I'd better scoot now – be good, Ray!"

All my love, Katarine

10.
The Caretaker's Lament

He felt most protective of the rich man's home. The new foreigners were beginning to come into the country, and not just the German and Russian businessmen who had never left, nor the diplomats all ensconced in the II Kerület, the Második Kerületen, the wealthy 2nd District. Now it was the Americans, too. Not that he had ever owned even a poor home, he had not. Nor did he have a wife and family. He was the older cousin of one of the workmen who spoke to the foreman. János was allowed to spend the nights here after the workmen had gone home. Lászlo had vouched for him, even though János was ruined by the cheap wine you could find in any state-run ABC grocery. He could be trusted. Everyone knew that even in these hills near the District 12 American School, it was not safe to leave a construction site unattended, and the builder let him stay on the property while it was being built. Once the underground wine cellar was roughed in, that is where he slept. At night, with the shape of the property that was being built against the steep hillside, he could listen to and hear the sounds from all directions.

Even scrap materials had to be protected, because when you had very little, you are able to make something out of not very much. János had no sympathy for the impoverished Russian soldiers who were not yet able to go home, they were sometimes present in these hills, too, though they were more sellers than pilferers, away from their poor bases. They would sell you any surplus item they could take from their base, especially anything with a sharpened blade.

This was not yet a home for a Hungarian, no, this was either for a rich westerner, or a diplomat, it was not yet the time for a Hungarian. This was for an individual who would be set up in comparative luxury by his company or by his government, while the workers he would soon employ would work for four hundred forints a day, less than two hundred dollars a month. To possess a car was out of reach for almost all, unless you were a manager at a high enough level for a company car, who would be happy to receive an old box Lada or a Dacia – at least it would not be a Trabant. Trabants were better suited for a person living near the Mátra, growing roots for the famous grape vines of Puttonyos Tokaji fame, and needing the open inside of the tiny combo to transport the living plants with cheap transportation.

There was still the anticipation of western wages, not like under the socialist system.

"We pretended to work, and they pretended to pay," they told us when we arrived.

This would be just one more disappointment that was yet to come.

No, this was not yet a house for a Hungarian, it was too soon since the wall came down, and there was not yet time for the wholesale selling off of state assets by those who knew their worth and how to acquire them. No, it was not yet a house for a Hungarian, it was still a time for the oligarchs, the diplomats, and the foreign businessmen. János did not know that neither would it continue to be a house for him to live at and to protect. When the house was completed, the rich foreigner told his driver, who told the construction manager, who told the foreman, who told the workman, and László told his cousin János, that he would have to find another place to live.

The ceremony took place between the buildings of the old industrial complex, one of country's largest industrial locations. All the management staff, functional leaders, and members of their teams were there, but excluded almost all of the factory workers who had been shepherded to new efficiency throughout the previous two years of change. There were few inefficient walking-around workers in the operations on his watch, and even today he would not allow his employees time off to attend the event to honor himself. He would not reduce the factory output even if just for an hour or two. This, for an event which had been approved not only by the Chairman and corporate headquarters, but by the local city government who had to agree to rename a street which ran through the factory property, the most-proud industrial company in the city and in the entire country. Within this compound, a long history extended from before both world wars, to a history which had now survived the last war of its twentieth century history, the cold war. The Wall and then the Curtain had fallen.

Today he was surrounded by colleagues, city officials, and friends. Among them included a former submarine commander, PhDs in science and history and finance, former professors, survivors of the 1956 revolution, those who had been denied university educations, and those who had crossed the border to leave and then returned. Employees from the UK, Austria, and a few visitors from America were in attendance. But most of all his local colleagues who had become friends, not of the kind that came to your home to visit and share a meal, but those who learned to love you through their shared humanity, the difficult history of the time, and the daily work together to build a future.

We exited from the eleven floors of the headquarters building, and walked through the car park set between the building just exited, the canteen to the right, and the factory to the left, past the engineering offices, the machinery development building, and other buildings still scarred by fifty-years-old war damage. We walked through the driveway between the buildings and turned left, then right and we made our way to a small street that bisected the buildings and led to the end of the street, to the properties edge, and to a locked gate that opened to Váci út.

It was a long walk back from the time I had arrived; from the day of this district IV celebration, to the time of my district XII arrival, where I first met him in this strange and beautiful country. It was a place where, when I first arrived at the Ferihegy airport, I could not even understand the pronunciation of the name of the company for which I had come to work. In the neighborhood surrounding the Panzió Guesthouse and Restaurant, at which we would live until the homes for our families were built or would become available for rent, I walked while I waited for him to return from the office to share with me my first evening in this country. I soon learned that all the gardens were fenced and gated, and all the dogs large and small whose barking followed me up and down the steep roads and walkways were safely enclosed behind those fences and gates. A rush to the edge of a property by a snarling and barking dog, ended behind the gate at the property line. You could tell the path a person walked if you followed the sound of barking dogs, a momentary aural trail left by each passing person, the sound of which marked the path of each step taken.

The sounds of the dogs circled the neighborhood around which I walked as I made my way back to the Panzió. I saw an old box Lada pull up to the curb on the street near the entrance. I watched a very large and very tall man untangle himself from the front seat of the small car and who, looking at me, smiled.

"Boy, am I glad to see you!" he exclaimed.

It was not long after those first days that a house was chosen by this large, tall man. János the caretaker felt protective of the new home which was still being built for this man, and he had begun to feel at home on the new property himself.

At the factory compound a new street sign was covered by a red, white, and green colored cloth. The CEO made a brief speech, standing beneath it on the corner of the small street that, though entirely within the property of our business, was recorded in the city street maps, and had become an official város utca, an official city street.

"Dear friends and colleagues," he began.

"We are gathered here today to honor a friend of this country, and a friend of this city, the city of my birth, a city from which I left as a young man, and returned a much older one. You all know that my mother lives here still, and never left, so although you may not consider me thus, she still considers me a young man, her boy, the son who has returned. Today we gather to honor a man, no longer a boy and not a young man, but a man who has given much to our company, to this city, and to the other towns and villages in which we operate, and to my native country as a whole. We all know that in his most difficult hours of that first year in which we began to work together, he never left us, or our city, or our country, and for that he will always be remembered and much loved."

"It has not been an easy time for this firm, and there are many fewer of us now than there were when we arrived, so the sacrifices have been many, and what was done was necessary for our survival. The largest part of these sacrifices was made in the operations he managed, but I think you will agree that none will fault Patrick for the way in which he dealt with the difficult actions which were necessary for our collective survival. He met adversity with fairness, and with as much care as possible, and he insisted that it be done with more care and consideration than that which was legally required."

"For the way in which he dealt with adversity both public and private, we make this declaration today, that hence forth, in the midst of this great company's headquarters, in this great capital city, this street shall bear his name, Patrick McGolvine utca."

The red, white, and green cloth, the colors of the national flag, was removed. It fell from the new street sign which had been installed between the buildings on the small street in which we now stood. It is a street surrounded by factory buildings and it leads to Váci út outside our compound, the street that leads directly through the heart of the city.

Patrick awoke with a start, something he had heard, something he had not heard before. He sat up in bed and could see the light casting a small parallelogram on the floor from beneath the bottom of the door across the hall. His wife was still watching the television that was a wonder in this part of the city where it was difficult to get a cable or a satellite dish installed. He sensed something wrong. It was a feeling he had thankfully not often felt since, but too many times had experienced it, when he was behind the lines in Korea, where he had commanded an artillery battery. Now he felt the fear again, the first in a long time more viscerally than he cared to remember, and for the first time in this new country in which he now lived and worked. He forced himself to lie back down, now hearing the muffled sound of the television in the next room.

"It was only the television," he told himself.

He lay back down and he did not know that something or someone was there as he fell back asleep.

When he awoke again, he sat up, and as he opened his eyes in the darkened room his brain was illuminated with a bright flash of light though the room was dark. In the delayed moment of recognition, he heard a noise like cracking wood. His chin had given way with the cleft and momentum of the first blow. Repeated blows broke the bridge of his nose, hit his forehead, and concussed his skull. Patrick instinctively brought up his right arm to ward off the next blow and the iron rod broke both the radius and ulna of his forearm as he cried out. He heard but could not see his wife.

"Patrick!" she screamed from the hallway.

She rushed into the room and jumped onto the back of the attacker, knocking him and the iron bar to the floor, her arms around his neck, wresting him down.

Patrick's mind was still illuminated by the flash of light and the fog of a concussion. He was unable to speak as his mouth did not work with the two halves of his jaw separated by the first blow, stunned by the concussion, and with a broken right arm. He slid to the floor beside his wife and sat on the back of his attacker. Patrick's two hundred thirty pounds pressed the attacker's seventy-five kilograms to the floor. His wife reached for and found the iron bar, and clubbed the attacker once on the head as she passed it to her husband's left hand. The attacker was subdued, defeated, and prostrate on the floor, and she recognized the face of the caretaker now lying on the floor of their bedroom, covered with both her husband's blood and his own.

"János!"

A hysterical call followed to the company's English-speaking security service, and the service and the police arrived as Patrick fought back the urge to lose consciousness.

"Jézus!" was all they said when they found Patrick atop the caretaker and he raised his face to try to look at them.

"Jesus, Mary, and Joseph!"

It was the only weary thought Patrick's mind managed to elicit when he saw the unfamiliar face of someone who stared back at him from the mirror in the bathroom before the ambulance arrived to take him to the hospital. His two jaws hung apart independently on each side of his face with a deep unnatural cleft in his chin. A knot the size of a golf ball emerged from his forehead above two blackened eyes. His lower forearm and right hand hung at an unnatural angle from the middle of his right arm. For this, the homeless caretaker would be remanded to a new and unpleasant home for many years.

If Patrick had been a State Department employee, or if he had been any other corporate executive, he would have awakened the next morning in a Zurich hospital, after a shuttle flight on a marine evacuation helicopter that would have departed from the roof of the American Embassy on Szabadság tér. But he was not a State Department employee, and Patrick would not allow the titanium braces to be screwed into his jaw outside of the capital city of this country. In a Zurich hospital, his bed would not have been in an open room in the common public wing of a Zentrum Kórház, a public inner-city hospital. The length of his six-foot-four-inch frame would not have hung over the end of a mattress. The skull series, the titanium braces and screws borrowed from a military hospital, the stitches for his wounds, and the set of the cast and the pins inserted into the bones of his right arm, all would have been performed in a Swiss hospital with the most modern technology. But Patrick was not a State Department employee, and he was not like any of the other corporate directors, and he still employed fourteen thousand workers who watched and waited and prayed for his recovery.

He did not know the future then, and he expected nothing more. He chose to recuperate in a bed too short for him in an open public ward. He would drink the beer smuggled in by me with a straw, which he had to insert between the titanium braces which would hold his jaw together for the rest of his life. He did not know then that he would fully recover, and by the grace of his strength and humility, a factory street in this great once and future city would bear his name.

11.
The Way to Luzon

We were in the last plane to take off from Elmore Field, February 10, 1945. The army had already completed the next airfield that we would use in Mangaldan, on the Island of Luzon. Mangaldan had been liberated from the Japanese, and later, when we had finished our work there, I would be in the last group to take off from that field as well. We were always the last to leave, after all of the war planes had been inspected. And we were now in-flight to the next airfield.

It took the entire runway to gain enough speed to become airborne, fully loaded, down the Elmore, one of two runways here on Mindoro Island. The Hiss Drome and Elmore Field had been built by army engineers in only thirteen days. The Marine's landing on the island had taken place on December 15, 1944, near San Jose and Mangarin Bay, in the southwest corner of the island at the edge of the town of San Roque. Ten days later, Christmas Day was a normal work day until the holiday dinner at 16:30, for the army engineers who were building the airfield. Before the end of the month both of the Mindoro Island runways were completed. The Elmore was ready for continuous dry weather operations three days after Christmas on December 28. Back in Leyte Island in the Philippines, at the airbase at Tanauan, it was my third Christmas away from home. We would arrive at this new base at the Elmore field on January 29, 1945 with our A-20 Havok's and B-24 Liberator's.

Sitting at the end of the runway, facing the wind, the pilots pushed the throttles forward on the twin 1,200 horsepower Pratt & Whitney radial engines of the C-47. The airplane shook, straining against the pull of the propellers in the humid tropical air. It was as if we were trying to escape from an overheated sauna whose doors were stuck shut. The plane bucked from side to side as the engines competed against the airframe braked solidly to the runway. The two powerful, unmuffled engines filled the interior of the aircraft with the roar of its fourteen-cylinder double-rowed radial engines, a tool of the war which carried men and supplies in sky-trains of destructive capability. The brakes were released against the straining of the engines, and the entire airframe shook at the moment of release as it began to roll with the 6,000lb payload of men and the implements of an air war. My jeep, the remaining airfield equipment and tools, and my inspection crew lifted off the runway to one more island on our long road home.

Once airborne we began to circle, gaining altitude in circle after circle after circle, to gain enough altitude to fly north and cross the High Rolling Mountains of central Mindoro. Mount Halcon rose off the starboard wing in the distance. Leaving the coast of the Island of Mindoro, we flew over Corregidor which lay at the entrance to Manila Bay. In less than a month the American flag would be raised there on March 3rd 1945.

The news about a new dive bomber appeared in the Coshocton Tribune on Oct 13, 1938, and I tore that page out of the newspaper and put it between the pages of the book I was reading for my senior year in high school, "The Last Shot," by Frederick Palmer. By the time I graduated, I knew I would leave the farm to have a different life. I decided that I would go to Columbus and study to become an airplane mechanic. It was one year before the invasion of Poland, the year of the Austrian Anschluss when Germany's eastern Reich, Austria, was finally brought together with the German master race, a dream of certain Austrians and almost all Germans since the year in which I was born, soon after the Great War was over, and our boys had returned home.

I thought about my plans every morning when I went to the barn to do my chores. My younger brother was still in school and I was sure he would not understand because of the hardship it would leave to him, and I did not dare mention it to my father, the smartest but most cruel farmer in the township. My mother would accept it with silence and suffering because she was still young enough to be bullied and cursed by my father, but I knew my sister would cry if she knew I was leaving. So, I talked to myself, as I tended the animals while I was alone in the stalls, or in the fields before my mother and brother and sister came out of the farmhouse to the barn to help with the milking. If I ever did speak aloud, I heard no grunt, or movement against the walls of a stall in protest, or the swishing of a tail in complaint about either the milking, or my leaving the farm. There was no one for me to talk to.

It would take more than two years before I was able to work up the courage to make this happen. I endured the beatings and verbal assaults that I knew would come as I tried to free myself from my father's domination and from the work that needed to be done on the farm seven days a week, winter, spring, summer, and fall. At my leaving the farm would lose the strongest, most experienced, and most responsible hand from the fields and barn, from the limestone quarry and the blacksmiths forge, and from the mechanic's garage. All of these activities made up the fabric of our livelihood. The one-hundred-eight-acre hill farm was at the center of our world. It was labor intensive work which left not much time for friends, or play, and just enough for study. My father would not release me until my younger brother was strong enough to take over the work I had done. I was his fourth beast of burden, after the three Percherons which rested in their stalls at the end of each day.

"Not until I'm able to buy a goddamned tractor," he constantly reminded me.

He would not say what my mother wanted to say, but dared not say to me.

He needed my back and my arms and my legs. And for two more years I was to milk and plow, plant and harvest, drill and blast, and harness and haul. By then a great storm rose in Europe, and my hopes would be sunk in the Pacific. I did not take my leave from our section twenty farm until after the war came. It changed all of that, and then it changed me.

One hundred and twenty years earlier, the patriarch of my mother's family was one of the first settlers in this area. He had come east from Pennsylvania, where the wilderness was already tamed, and neighbors were set in place. He went west to Ohio, again in search of open land and no close neighbors. Indians would not leave the area for many years to come, a time when fences were still unknown and the Indians let their horses graze across an open countryside. Perry Township was surveyed and named for the Commodore hero of the Battle of Lake Erie, in the War of 1812. Fifty years later came the Civil War of the Rebellion, and in another fifty years the first of the Great Wars.

I was swept up into the new world in December 1941, after we listened to the President's declaration of war, which we listened to on our Atwater Kent radio, its antenna wire strung from the barn to the house. I made my plans to leave for the war before the government could make its plans for me. My father could have no voice in this action. He was a man who had never allowed his own life to be detained and wasted by a government war. He could lay claim to be the sole support of an extended family. He did not leave during WWI, when he was a young man in his father's blacksmith shop which he hated, and he would never leave the farm now. I enlisted the day after the New Year holiday, and left the farm two days later on January 4th, 1942, never to return to live and to work on any farm again.

We disembarked from the troop train and entered the station in Savannah, Georgia. Separate white and colored drinking fountains greeted us on the rail siding at the station. My unit was activated there, and my sensibilities were confused with the open segregation of the South which frightened me. I had seen the segregation of the North when I helped my father sell potatoes on the city streets of Canton. Northern separation of the races was nearly as complete, but the cruel and open segregation I witnessed in Savannah was with a viciousness and danger more severe than that which I had ever witnessed in the north, and even greatly exceeded the rural cruelty inflicted by my father on my mother, and on my siblings, and on me.

We completed our training there, and later in DeRidder, Louisiana, and then left the south behind to travel west. I developed a seething contempt for ninety-day wonders, when a Lieutenant admonished me after an all-night passage, on a rail siding without water.

"Get yourself a shave, soldier!"

I scraped off my dry overnight beard and we continued, riding on an overcrowded troupe train to California and the Mohave Desert. Our destination was Rice Army Airfield, and it's two 5,000ft runways.

While we trained in the desert, the Bismarck Sea Battle raged in the South Pacific. Two Japanese warships were sunk, and six other ships were damaged at Kavieng. Men died and drowned as we slept on the tarmac in America under the wings of the planes we studied and on which we worked. We tried to escape the desert heat and scorpions by sleeping under the planes as we prepared for battles already taking place in the South Pacific. We dreamed and dreaded the water crossing to come as we sweated and suffered, studied and trained in the heat of the California desert. Soon enough, I would learn what real heat and a suffocating humidity was, exchanging desert scorpions for leeches, mosquitoes, malaria, and skin ailments in the heat and humidity of the South Pacific.

On November 1, 1943, the SS Nieuw Amsterdam sailed with 6,800 troops from San Francisco to Wellington, New

Zealand. We sailed for eleven days across the North Pacific Ocean, to the South Pacific, and entered the Southern Pacific Ocean to reach New Zealand. On arriving at the Port of Wellington we left the ship, two men abreast, to stretch our legs and circle the entire town. We crossed the central Pipitea district, and circled through Thorndon, Wadestown, and Northland districts. Men, women, and children came out to watch us march around the circumference of the city, offering food and fresh fruit in exchange for our US dollars. By the time the first column of men returned to the ship, the last men were just leaving it for their walkabout around the city. From Wellington it was a three-day voyage to Sydney, Australia, where we arrived on November 19, 1943.

I had already been in the 5th Army Air Force for almost two years.

During the next month we moved overland in Australia to Camp Moorooka at Brisbane, and to Armstrong Paddock at Townsville where we departed on the Liberty Ship SS Anson Burlingham to arrive at Port Moresby, New Guinea, four days before Christmas on December 21, 1943.

For most of the next year we operated our airfields in New Guinea. In January 1944 we moved to Gusap. The 54th Troop Carrier Wing of the 5th Army Airforce took my 388th Squadron over the 13,000ft Owen Stanley Mountains. The main runway for the 312th Bomb Group at Gusap was a 6,000ft long surface of interlocking steel Marston mats, ten feet long by fifteen-inch pierced steel planks, weighing sixty-two and one-half pounds each. From Gusap we transferred to Nadzab, off the Highlands Highway in the Marobe Province of the Markham Valley.

The war did not wait for us to settle in. On June 29, 1944, soon after we arrived in Nadzab, 1st Lieutenant Billy Hollingshead, and tail gunner Staff Sergeant Leonard Tilden, Jr. of our 388th Fighter Bomber Squadron were lost on a raid against Yakamul Village, west of Wewak. We searched the jungle for several days but found no trace of the plane or the men. Almost thirty years later, the wreckage of their A-20 would finally be found in 1973.

From July 4th until November 13th, we operated out of Hollandia, New Guinea. Then the 388th Squadron sailed on Liberty Ships, LSTs, and other vessels 1,500 miles to arrive at Leyte Island in the Philippines on November 19. Two months later on January 29, 1945 we arrived at Mindoro Island.

We left Elmore Field on Mindoro Island on February 10, 1945. Six days later on February 16, our A-20's and B-24's supported the paratroopers on Corregidor from our new base on the Island of Luzon at Mangaldan. Our A-20's were ordered to make low altitude bombing and strafing runs. My aircraft technical inspections for the A-20 twin engine dive bombers were known to be tough, the airplanes had to be right up. I wrote up a lot of things on these aircraft, and some of the inspections and maintenance items were tough to get at. But that wasn't my problem. Because of this I did not have many friends, but I did what I had to do. The mechanics didn't always appreciate the extra work they had to do on my watch. But after a near fatal cockpit fire, my request to move the position of the escape axe from behind the pilot to a position below his left arm was approved by the chain of command. The thanks I received from the first pilot to escape from the jammed canopy of a burning A-20 using the repositioned axe was thanks enough for me, over the complaints of the extra work from my inspection crew.

I won't forget the sight of Corregidor when we flew over Manilla Bay on the way to Mangaldan. Men were dying beneath us while the island fortress was rocked with artillery and gun ship explosions, softening up the Japanese defenders for the paratroopers who were to land there on the 16th of February with our close-in support. We did not know how many more men would die, how many more pilots and planes we would lose on what we knew would be our bloody march to Tokyo. Decades later, unclassified After-Action Reports documented the cruel fact of war, and the manner in which only 50 Japanese soldiers of nearly seven thousand survived the island assault, against our 207 dead and 684 wounded. Although we incurred many times fewer losses than the Japanese, too many Americans died, and if you saw one of your planes crash on a runway return, witnessed an A-20 drop into the sea, or knew of a plane that was lost in a jungle crash, the images both seen and imagined never left you.

After almost one month in Mangaldan, one of our young officers decided we should fill-in our unused foxholes. But on March 1st, an air raid by several Mitsubishi G4M2's took place, a land attack bomber that we called the "Betty". Some of the men were thrown out of their cots with the concussive effect of the exploding bombs. None of the Betty's scored a direct hit on our bivouac area near the grounds of the airfield, but trenches and foxholes reappeared quickly before there was time for the countermanding order to be given, to dig them back out again.

From Mangaldan we flew to the airfield at Floridablanca. Our B-24 was so loaded up that we had to take turns standing on the catwalk over the open bomb bay doors, less than a foot wide, that separated the fore and aft compartments. With a fuselage two times the size of a C-47, the bomb bays were side by side in the high wing, four-engine boxcar of a plane. I don't know why the bomb bay doors were rolled open, no one explained and we did not ask. We did what we were told. It was April 16, 1945, we were sixty miles northwest of Manilla, the recaptured city into which our troops had entered less than three months earlier. They raised the American flag there with McArthur on March 7, 1945.

The Luzon Campaign would be over in June. In August the atomic bombs were dropped on Hiroshima and Nagasaki. Russia would declare war on Japan, with the final Japanese surrender in September. After almost two years of sweating-it-out in the south Pacific, my unit left Floridablanca in October

1945 on the troopship Cape Canso, and arrived at the mouth of the Columbia River at Portland, Oregon on November 9, 1945.

All of that was yet to come and we did not know what the war would bring to us. Each battle brought us closer to the island of Japan, and the knowledge that there would be a fight to the death on that island. There were rumors of a million casualties if we did not end the war before we crossed the 35th parallel on the way to Tokyo.

The 706th Tank Battalion disembarked from San Francisco on March 22, 1944 and arrived at Hawaii on April 29th. The Battalion shipped from Hawaii on LSTs to support Admiral Chester Nimitz's wing of the Pacific Island-Hopping Campaign. The 706th was on Guam by July 22, 1944 and arrived at the Philippines on November 23rd. Six companies of the 706th Tank Battalion landed at Dulag Beach, and disembarked from their LSTs to defend the coastline of Leyte Gulf. It was comprised of HQ Company, Service Company, and Companies A, B, C, D. In the 3rd platoon of Company B, my cousin, Tech 5 Corporal Herald Rider, a tank gunner, arrived and moved off the beach to bivouac near Tarragona, in the area south of Dulag. His unit was temporarily attached to the 306th Regimental Combat Team infantry division. The 306's RCT was positioned only thirty kilometers from where I was stationed at Tanauan Airdrome with the 312th Bomb Group. Two days later, after Thanksgiving, Company B was relieved from attachment to the 306th and reverted to the 706th Tank Battalion to set up a beach defense for HQ company. Harold received permission to visit me a few days later, and we would talk about how far we had come from the farms of central Ohio to the jungles of the south pacific, to fight on our way to Tokyo, and to the end of the war.

Rider had the worst sense of direction of any man I've ever known, but as a gunner in the tanks corps it did not matter. When the time of our brief visit was over, I was to drive him back to his unit in the jeep that was assigned to me as an A-20 crew chief, and we proceeded south on the Tacloban-Baybay highway. Herald directed me onto the La Paz-Mayorga Road, six miles north of the correct turn-off which should have been the road to Tarragona.

We had not traveled far on La Paz before a soldier from the 306th came out of the jungle on the left side of the road and stopped us.

"Just where the hell do you two assholes think you are going?"

He challenged us with a lowered rifle, blocking the road more effectively than with a lowered gate.

"To the 706th at Tarragona," Herald replied.

"I'm Corporal Rider, tank gunner, Company B, 3rd platoon."

"This is the Javier-Abuyog Road, isn't it? This here is my cousin, Crew Chief Master Sergeant Neldon from the 388th Bomb Squadron with the 312th up at Tanauan."

"Jesus Christ, corporal," snapped the sergeant, "this is fucking enemy territory."

"Turn the hell around and get back to T-Baybay Road and make a right. Head south ten clicks to Javier-Abuyog after crossing two streams and then make another right and go west. You've gone too far if you come to Bito Lake, and you'll be lucky if the Japs don't shoot you. If you are captured and not killed, you'll get one dirty rice ball a day, and not enough water. It will be your breakfast, lunch, and supper."

"Sergeant, you!" he commanded, and pointed to me behind the steering wheel of the jeep.

"Take this corporal back to his outfit and get your sorry ass the hell back to the 388th before dark, or you might be one dead GI."

Years and a lifetime later, both of us surviving the war, my cousin Herald could get lost in any small town. He visited me dozens of times at my home less than thirty miles from where he lived, and each time he would call for directions after wandering about through the wrong streets. He could not navigate with or without maps for places he did not visit every day. But when he was in the 706th, it did not matter. Other men drove and navigated the Shermans.

He told me that they were trained to look for the bunker slits in the sand mounds with their 75mm tank guns on the islands where they fought. He said one day they fired a high explosive round into a sand dune bunker and one of the Japanese soldiers inside survived the blast. Somehow, he was thrown out by the explosion, and lay stunned on the sand, helpless.

"It looked like he was trying to say something but of course we could not hear anything through the noise inside the tank and the explosions of the battle outside. He tried to get up and managed to raise himself off the sand just as we fired a .30 caliber burst into him, which took off one of his legs at the hip. The femoral artery squirted its contents onto the sand and he fell on his side, spun around from the impact of the rounds. When the burst tore through him, it rolled him backwards and his arms flung out like the ribbons on a maypole."

It had been only yesterday, but now it was forty years later when he told me this at one our family picnic reunions.

"We had to do these things," he said to me quietly in a flat voice without any of the emotion that was still repressed since the war and that day long ago, just one of many of the days on the islands in the South Pacific.

"But I still remember."

Herald was the 75mm turret gunner on his tank's five-man team. For what he saw and for what he had to do, I never criticized him for the rest of his life, especially after that day at Tanauan and Tarragona, nor for any of the times that he got lost back home when he came to visit me.

Forty years ago. It is 1944 again.

Tonight, when I get back to camp after I returned my cousin to the 706th, I return my jeep, go through the line at the mess, and enter my tent at the end of the day. I finally sit down on the edge of my army cot, and I can't control the shaking in my arms and legs and hands, as I remove my clothes and boots and carefully draw the mosquito netting around me.

There would have been no such comfort, as harsh as it sometimes seemed here, in a Japanese prisoner of war camp in the jungles of Leyte, where we fought on our way to Luzon and to the end of the war.

12.
The Indians

The road which wound through the hills above Deertown was called Nudeltown Hill. Some of the Swiss immigrants who settled here said that the rolling hills surrounding the highest point of the county reminded them of the western regions of the Bern Canton and the foothills of the Jura Mountains. Many decades later, it was paved and renamed a much nicer sounding Mount Blessed Road. No one remembers why the name was changed, perhaps it was because of the enormous mansion and estate that would occupy the hundreds of acres of reclaimed strip-mined land at the highest point of the road, with the best views of the valley in any direction. From here were the only views of the valley, because the road in either direction from the estate was bordered on both sides by scrub trees, thorn bushes, and blackberry bushes which grew wild over all the unreclaimed strip-mined land. No one ever bothered to pick the berries any more.

The name Mount Blessed, sounded better, more suitable, more twenty-first century, now reclaimed from the environmental carelessness of the twentieth century. In that century, the coal stripped from these hills, still fed the local brick furnaces, two steel yards, and the light plant with its three coal-powered electrical generators, and in turn fed all the businesses that supported and fabricated the goods that made Main Street, and the banks, and thousands of jobs possible. Now the Mount was reclaimed by the newly conspicuous descendants of the old rich who had built the original town.

Nudeltown Hill rose behind tiny and modest Deertown, a poor looking one-street neighborhood now surrounded by corn fields on one side of the main highway, a junk yard, and the over-the-road trucks parked on the other. It wasn't always so.

During the depression years, before the highways of the military industrial complex were built by the president who railed against them, there was a stable of a sort where a young man named Johnny could keep a horse. It was not just any horse. It was a proud Tennessee Walker. Another young man named Clarence on the high school baseball team spent hours strengthening his wrists by batting countless cinder stones picked up from between the ties of the railroad tracks which ran behind the town. But eventually Nudeltown Hill sounded so 1930's, so depression era rough, that the name was no longer good enough. The road was paved, the mansion built, and the old names were forgotten. The new name, Mount Blessed Road, corrected all that. It was an address that was fine enough to hang your name on a shingle without embarrassment, and it hung from the enormous gate at the entrance to the estate. It opened to a winding lane which made its way across wood-fenced pastures, and finally circled around the columned entrance of the main residence. It was an unintended fatuitous consequence, that the folks attending the tiny Baptist church on the way up from Deertown, across the railroad tracks and at the top of the first bend in the road, would no longer need to be careful about getting dust on their Sunday morning and Wednesday evening clothes, which used to be kicked up on the road which lay beside the church parking lot before it was paved.

Clarence and Johnny both had 1925 Indian Scouts with 37 cubic inch engines. The engines and gearboxes of these motorcycles were bolted together, and gears drove the wheels, not chains. Both of them rode without helmets, goggles, or gloves, and you could hear them coming while they were still out of sight. They rode through the decade of the 30's on their Indian's, played basketball and baseball, hunted in the wooded hills, rode horses, fished, swam in the river that flowed through the town, and they knew that war was coming, too.

Where it descended into Deertown, the Indians roared through the clouds of dust on the unpaved dirt road. They roared down Nudeltown Hill, through a one-street Deertown, and out onto the main paved highway, split in two by the rails of streetcar tracks that ran all the way to the nearest town and on to the county seat beyond.

There is a picture of Clarence by the old tavern store on the main highway, taken on his final home leave before he was sent by the army to England. He could speak German, one of the languages spoken by his immigrant parents at home, and in it he was smiling beneath the clean sharp brim and peak of his army service cap, profile to the camera so you could see the sergeant stripes on his sleeve. He signed the photograph with a flourish and gave it to his favorite sister.

Three years later, when the fighting was almost over, Clarence crossed the channel to make his way to Germany with the 116th Signal Radio Intelligence Company to help the liberation of the concentration camps, and the interrogation of guards and prisoners. In one more week, VE Day would be declared. The first camp he was sent to on April 29, 1945, was in a wooded area at the edge of a town, a former artists colony, which had been cleared and walled for a labor camp several years before the war. When you entered the headquarters of the camp, the SS buildings and offices were neat and clean, and you were left with the impression of a prosperous, successful operation. But as you left behind the headquarters buildings, and passed through the main camp gate, you crossed to the assembly grounds between the prisoner barracks and maintenance building, and to the right another camp entrance where, on the top of an elaborate iron gate was spelled out the camp motto. The euphemistically named "maintenance" building was painted a light cheerful yellow, the same color of the formal SS buildings, but the insides of which remained marked, and scarred, and ugly. Maintenance performed in this building included survival experiments to determine how long a man could survive in freezing water, or the effect of poisons ingested by children.

A wooded path behind the barracks led to a handsome brick building with a massive central chimney. A beautifully paved cobblestone courtyard surrounded a large stone fountain. A narrow winding path through the woods behind it led to an exposed brick wall against which prisoners, condemned to death for special offenses, were shot. Others were hung from ropes or strangled on hooks alongside and within view of the cremation furnaces which were contained within the handsome brick building, where, after their hanging or strangulation, their bodies would be burned.

Clarence had been a minor league baseball player.

"A good prospect. Any consideration shown him will be appreciated," wrote Cy Young and Kid Elberfeld from Hot Springs, Arkansas in a signed recommendation note given to Clarence in 1939, after he attended their baseball school in nearby Dover.

He played one season for the St Louis Cardinals farm team, but his shoulder gave out on a throw from third base, and then the war took what was left.

Clarence left the prison camp after he was done with the evacuation of the former inmates, now released. The SS guards who survived being shot on the first day of the chaotic liberation were now themselves imprisoned. There is another picture of him after he left the camp, carrying a worn ditty bag in his left hand, sharp creases in his forehead, standing on the corner of a ruined building below a street sign which said "Dachauerstraße." In this picture, he is looking back towards the camera over his left shoulder, unsmiling, smaller looking, leaner, weary, wearing a worn wool olive-colored garrison cap, somewhere in northwest Munich in early May 1945.

Johnny waited for Clarence in the hallway each afternoon before they went to dinner in the tiny dining hall, really just an open corner by the nurse's station, which they always entered together. Now, at ninety-three years old, Johnny was several years younger than his old friend Clarence who would be 100 on his next birthday, and they sat at the dinner table together, always Johnny to the left, and Clarence on the right. Each night after dinner Johnny walked down to where Clarence bunked, said goodnight, and then went back down the hall to his own room. Clarence always waited and watched until Johnny returned to stand by his own door, and they would signal to each other that they were OK, waving handkerchiefs to each other to make it easier to see from the opposite ends of the floor where they lived. When you lived together in tight quarters, you became friends with the ones with whom you had something in common. The funny thing was, you could never tell who would get along and who would become friends. Sometimes during the war men grouped together with those whom you would never believe could become friends. Sometimes opposites would introduce sisters to buddies and become brothers-in-law for the rest of their lives, not just brothers in spirit, fighting together during the war. But Clarence and Johnny had known each other their whole lives, both before, during, and after, the war.

The two elderly gentlemen were the most physically active of the men who lived on the floor, and they still shared an athletic presence that made them comfortable with each other, even in old age. Clarence would be Johnny's last friend here at the home, the last of the Indian riders.

The USS Maryland, "Mighty Mary" to her shipmates, was damaged during the Pearl Harbor attack, and afterwards it was towed back to the Puget Sound Naval Yard where she was repaired in two months. The thirty-five-thousand-ton Colorado class battleship was returned to duty in the South Pacific in June 1942. It carried eight 16inch Mark 1 guns in four double turrets, twelve 5inch guns, and four 3inch guns. Two 21inch torpedo tubes were below the water line. She was the first battleship in US history to carry 16inch guns. During the Pacific War she would also be fitted with forty Bofors 40mm anti-aircraft guns in quad mounts, twenty-four 28mm guns in six quadruple mounts, forty-eight 20mm guns, and eighteen mounted .50 caliber machine guns.

Johnny was a range finder operator for both the 5inch guns and the 40mm Bofors. He was with the Maryland when she sustained torpedo damage during the Battle of Saipan, and also when she took her first kamikaze hit at the Battle of Leyte Gulf. She suffered a second kamikaze hit during the Battle of Okinawa, crashing into the top of Turret No. 3. The two 16inch guns were undamaged, but the 20mm mounts were destroyed, and fire ignited the 20mm ammunition. Ten men died, thirty-seven were wounded, and six were missing and never found. Johnny was among the wounded that day at Okinawa, April 7, 1945. He lost the hearing in his left ear when thrown from his battle station from one of the 5inch guns. One of his gunner mates was killed when his body was severed by shrapnel from the Japanese kamikaze, but Johnny had been thrown clear of any projectiles released from the crash or from the explosions which followed.

When he hitchhiked home from Seattle after the war, Johnny had trouble hearing whenever he rode shotgun, and always had to cock his head to the side enough so that his right ear could hear what the driver had to say.

He worked on the Wooster railroad for the rest of his life. He married, had three children, and won three horseshoe championships in the area, and never again spoke about the war unless you asked.

When Clarence died, Johnny lost the last friend he had to talk to. Now he walked down the hall by himself when he went for dinner, and there was no one to wave a white handkerchief at, to let him know that he was OK before he went into his room each night. Now he had to satisfy himself with the occasional talk among visitors, who might sit at his dinner table when they came to visit someone else at the home.

One day, one of the regular visitors got him talking about the war and the Indian motorcycles he used to ride with his friend Clarence. He had already learned that when you talked to Johnny, you had to remember to come around to his right side.

13.
The Fat Man and D-Day

Roger stood about five-foot-six, and weighed one hundred ninety-five pounds. When he was younger, he stood almost five foot eight and weighed one hundred forty-five pounds, about average for a man born in the nineteen twenties. It was not just because of his age that he was beginning to lose height and physical strength of all kinds. It was also because the extra weight he now carried compressed the cartilage between his vertebrae and he suffered from low back pain. He had lost at least an extra inch as his weight increased over the years. With the weight and with the effect of the ever-present cigarettes that he smoked, he moved with difficulty and had to favor his right leg. I was his new, younger neighbor. It was obvious to me that he lacked self-discipline and had let himself go. He did not seem to mind the effect of the extra weight so much as what he would have missed if he had altered his diet, and made an effort to keep it off.

His wife Rita was an excellent cook. She liked to spoil him with simple things, like sweetened lemonade when it was hot and he was working outdoors, and a glass of red wine at any time of the year when he was done with his work. She would bring the iced lemonade to him in a glass if he was working in the yard, or in a thermos if he was on his way to the golf course.

Roger did not have an open face, his eyes were too small for that, and he carried a perpetual squint, partially due to his fair complexion and light blue eyes, and what remained of blonde hair atop his head, but also because he was the kind of man who was a constant skeptic. Not out of bitterness or suspicion – he believed in the basic goodness of men – but he wanted to be sure, and he did not suffer airs or foolishness lightly. He was always friendly, or perhaps I should say, civil. He was approachable, not in an off-putting way. But he was not open in a friendly way, and even after you got to know him, he was not a warm, embraceable sort of fellow for anyone but Rita, and there was never a public display of affection between them. Perhaps it was a cultural shyness and because she still spoke, after so many years, with a heavy Italian accent.

You might want me to say that his house and yard were as neat as a pin, but they were not. They were neat enough, but not excessively and noticeably neat enough to stand out. If there was a storm that left branches and leaves on the ground from the white oaks that stood in his yard, Roger would be outside the next day for the clean-up, but not obsessively so. Some men nearly sweep their lawns with a broom and will pick individual weeds out of the grass. I once knew a man who worked six days a week at a small restaurant he owned, and on the seventh day each week he spent Sunday mornings cleaning the place. Sunday afternoons found him in his yard or scouring the inside of his home, the most obsessively clean man I ever knew. He was also one of the most open and friendly men I ever knew, though in an almost formal kind of way from years of serving customers with his wife, who was a constant, cheerful companion at work and at home. They were inseparable. But this was not Roger, and you rarely saw his wife, but when you did see her around the house they were usually together. He knew how to do just enough and a little more, and they always seemed to be happy together.

I was in the early years of my career, and I viewed Roger as a nice, simple man, my father's age, comfortable to be around because there was no need of spending too much time in cultivating a relationship. We were simply acquaintances, neighbors, and we said our hellos, and how is it going, and once in a while we might briefly talk about something important like the kind of paint I should use inside my house, and whether the siding on my house was heavy and dense enough to rest on the foundation securely. These were comfortable things to speak about because we did not have to invest any emotion or feeling. He was overweight, and like the caricature of an older suburban man, he sat atop his riding mower when he mowed his small yard. His stomach reached to the steering wheel. He would ride and never walk when he cut the grass, and the small but perceptible limp in his right leg was because I knew he had comfortably let himself go, and his knee hurt. He could ride and not have to walk in the yard. In other words, a very nice man, a comfortable suburbanite that I would live beside for five years. I never entered more than a few feet into his yard or driveway. I never stepped a foot inside his home, nor he in mine.

We had been neighbors for almost three years when he began to talk one day.

"Certain things never bothered me," he said, "though some men could not take the pressure. I was able to let it roll off my back," he told me one afternoon in early June, when we had both finished with our yard work.

That was the way he always was when we talked together about anything, when the weather was nice and I had time to stand for a few minutes and talk. He understood that with two young children you never had much time. He was never up nor down when I saw him, always the same, never happy or sad, though he seemed somewhat satisfied, and he never complained about things, not even politics. I traveled a lot, and he seemed interested in the places I had been. It had been obvious to me that he had not been to very many places, except to Florida with Rita a few times when they could afford it. Though I was his son's age, he seemed to enjoy listening to me when I spoke about the places I had been, and I enjoyed the telling to him. He seemed to try to discern if I could take the pressure in the current position that I held, which I was sure carried more responsibility than any job he had ever had in his entire blue-collar life. I think I passed the test with him. He said he appreciated the way I cared for my family, and then we would talk about paint or carpentry, or how often the mower needed sharpening in order to cut the lawn properly without tearing the blades of grass and damaging them.

It surprised me greatly then, after I had moved away to begin a new even more responsible position, that I received a call from my former neighbor. I had not been long in my new home, and the move away from Roger and Rita had taken place in the autumn. By now I had another child, a third child they had never seen, and they said they wanted to visit.

But it was that afternoon in early June before the summer solstice, that Howard sat down on the low brick wall which separated my driveway from his yard. I sat down beside him and he began to talk.

"If I had been in the first wave, I would probably not have survived," he paused, taking a drag on his cigarette, "but I was in the second wave, C-company at Dog White, and I made my way to the beach, untouched, through the blood and the bodies in the water, and then onto the beach. By the end of the day, the machine gun emplacements on the cliffs were finished."

"Then we moved off the beach, while the GRC platoons began removing the dead. It would take three days, and the medics still attended to the wounded and the dying."

He said this with no emotion, and looked down and smoked his cigarette. He looked out in the direction over the yard as he spoke, looking downward then up again every time he pulled on the cigarette, not focusing on what he could see in front of him. He was looking into memory as he spoke, looking out over a beach forty years ago, with the sea to his back, the cliffs above, and into the fields beyond which he could still not yet see, that were beyond the beach. He heard the sounds of metal piercing the air, of metal hitting metal, sand, sea, and flesh. The dull ring of metal, the spitting sound against the sand, the slapping and bubbling sound of the water, and the agony of men who were wounded and dying.

"There was a lot of fear and a lot of anger, and then we found out what a hedgerow was."

Roger and his wife had come to see my youngest son, who was born a few days after we moved. Now we were no longer neighbors and they had never seen him. He and his wife settled into the upholstered furniture of our family room, and he liked the view out the window to the tall trees, much like the ones we had left in the old neighborhood. He approved. The baby's nap was over, coffee had been drunk, and the cups and saucers removed as my wife went to bring the child for our visitors who had come to see the miracle of another generation. It was peaceful in the countryside where we lived. The only battles for me were safely waged in offices and on factory floors.

"You couldn't know how you would react in combat," he told me that summer afternoon in June.

"Some guys could take the stress and function, while others, whom you might have thought to be the toughest sons-of-bitches, might freeze and cry, unable to move, or shoot, or follow orders. They had to be forced to react. You had to drag them and throw them along until they were able to join the fight. You couldn't tell," he said, always with a cigarette in his hand.

The smoke curled between his sentences.

"But the stuff never bothered me, and I don't know why, it just didn't. Some of the guys would ask me how or why I could let it roll off my back. I didn't have an answer for them."

Rita and my wife left the room to go into the kitchen with the baby and the other two children. Roger asked me how work was going, and if I had any financial issues with the move, the new house, and the baby. He was that kind of neighbor and friend, even though he was my father's age and a generation older than me. The war of our summer conversation was over decades before, mentioned only once on that day, and now sitting here with Roger in our comfortable home, I thought again of what he had told me that day in June.

"After we came off the beach I was shot in the neck. We were fired on by the Germans while we crossed a field after cutting our way through and around one of the hedgerows bordering it. Lucky as hell, just a graze wound that didn't slow me down. It just didn't bother me. I could take it. One of the guys in my unit cracked up and had to be evacuated. Don't know what happened to him, it was not pretty to see, and you didn't want him to upset the rest of the squad."

"We couldn't get through the hedgerows, and the Germans were trying to retreat. They made defensive lines behind them, but we eventually surrounded them and attacked them from the front and the rear of their positions, and we eventually killed all of them. They didn't have a chance, poor bastards. There was a lot of killing on both sides. We shed no tears for them."

"Later, crossing France, I took three machine gun bullets above and on both sides of the knee of my right leg. It put me to the ground with a hairline fracture, but I did not lose my leg. I had to continue to fight as best I could until later that day. You lived and died by inches or seconds in combat. A bullet had grazed my neck in the hedgerows near the beach, and now three machine gun bullets which broke but did not cause me to lose my leg in southern France."

"I evacuated to an army medical hospital on the Ligurian Sea at Livorno until I recovered, because the war was not over for me. I thanked God the food was good, and the Italian nurses were pretty. I was ready when I was ordered, to rejoin my unit in time for the goddamned miserably cold fight in the Ardennes in December. We didn't know then to call it the Bulge."

These were the things he had told me in June of that long-ago summer. Now it was fall, and Roger and his wife Rita said goodbye after their Sunday afternoon visit to our new home. It was the last time I would ever see Roger, now an older, heavier, comfortable, suburban, remitted, pensioned, old man.

Outside of my home he lit one more cigarette, and walked to his car with a slight, almost imperceptible limp in his right leg.

14.
The Playing Field

Drew was the strongest friend I ever had.

On summer days after work, we drove home in his BMW 2002 and he would drop me off to change clothes. We would meet later at the Lott Courts which lay between the old Hutch gym and the football field, a short walk from my 34th Street apartment. We liked to play on "center" court, the one with the bleachers next to it where the best school matches were played. He out-weighed me by at least twenty pounds of muscle, even though I stood an inch taller than him. His method of warming up before we began to hit balls was to drop to the court and do fifty push-ups. He was physically stronger than me in every way, but he was new to tennis, and I had played many years at a higher skill level than he had been able to acquire since he stopped playing lacrosse. He had been offered a professional contract, but at four thousand dollars a season, it was not enough to make lacrosse the start of a career.

We played so hard, and he hit the balls with such force, that the smack of the balls could be heard beyond the courts, and students would walk over and sit on the bleachers to watch the play of a slender player on one side who kept the ball in play and moved it around on the court, returning shots with not quite the power but with more accuracy than the massively built young man on the other side. When they arrived to the sounds and seated themselves on the bleachers, they saw the sculpted physique of a less skillful player, so strong that the watching was as much about the picture of his strength as the length of the rallies. The competition between us was a slugfest of skill versus raw power.

It was a long way from Choate, a longer way from Sandtown, to the tennis courts in this Ivy League neighborhood.

We often had dinner together at the west end of the university for bluefish and mussels – if the waitress said they were not too sandy. The fare reminded Drew of the Bay where he grew up. But he had never eaten this seafood in a restaurant or tavern when he lived there. It would have been cooked by his mother or grandmother in the apartment in which they lived, taken straight from the docks. When he talked about these things he sometimes laughed quietly, and many times it was this mannerism that gave you the impression that he was always surprised, diffident, reserved about the way things turned out. He sometimes looked up at you without completely raising his face, and he needed to furrow his eyebrows slightly to be able to lift his eyes to meet your gaze. He was powerfully built, but he was also as quiet as he was strong. He could never quite believe he had gone from the streets of his neighborhood to the prep school of presidents, then to an Ivy League University, and now a Fortune 500 company.

We paid the bill and went outside. It was cooler on the street now. A bus loaded with passengers stopped at the corner and a few descended to the street. Two men who lived on the street and slept in abandoned buildings and doorways sat on a step and silently inspected the people going by. Down the street a siren whistled and an ambulance sped to the nearby hospital. Students walked by carrying books and discussions, coming from late classes and the libraries. The light changed, stopping traffic, and we crossed the street to the other side.

"When I was growing up, I hung around with a group of older guys," he explained.

"I don't know why, I just did."

"Some were four or five years older than me," he continued, "and it seemed like wherever they went, trouble followed, and it happened."

A beautiful girl crossed the street as we left the Bluefish Tavern at Market and 40th, long since now replaced by a sushi bar and modern university townhomes. She was singing to herself in a high sweet voice, jet black hair falling over her shoulders and down her back.

"It happened in an empty field not far from the neighborhoods where we lived. It was a pretty big field and we used to play a lot of ball games in it. A busy road ran beside it and you could hide in the field so that you could not be seen from the road, or from the service station on the other side. One of the older guys was hiding in the field that night."

The old Conoco gas station was at the intersection of Washington and Monroe, across from the one-hundred-twenty-acre park, a nine-hole golf course at one end of it. The old mansion was now the only remnant of the buildings that a twenty-three-hundred-acre plantation had once held. Not even a scar on the hill remained where the slave quarters had stood. The long forgotten shamanistic rituals of African intermediaries had taken place there, and would not be rediscovered for one more decade after that night, not until a chunk of clear quartz was discovered in the ground. It was a piece of African quartz used by a shaman who had witnessed the blood of slaves that lived and died on those grounds for almost two hundred years.

The last customer came into the station at dusk, as the golfers left the course to go home. At twenty cents per gallon, a fill-up only cost four dollars, and there was never more than twenty or thirty dollars in the cash register that had not yet been deposited into the safe.

Drew entered the gas station and went to the soft drink machine beside the door to the garage bay. He was a clean-cut young man with a shy demeanor, handsome, with impeccable manners. Hop was seventeen, and unknown to Drew, lay hidden in the field across the road and looked to see that no one else came into the station when the lights on the pumps went out. At thirteen years of age, boys are already on their way to becoming strong young men, and Drew was already known to be very strong.

"Hey mister, I just want a Coke, been caddying all day, and I need to get home before my mama starts to worry about me."

"Help yourself and get a move on, son, it's time to close up and get home. Another dime in the machine don't make no difference to me."

The attendant opened the cash register to take out the last of the bills and change. He put them into a bank cash deposit bag with the receipts. At the end of each day, he dropped the bag into the slot at the top of the safe. At the end of each day, the owner would be by to take the receipts of the day to the bank. As he put the money and the receipts into the bag, Hop entered the station with a .22 caliber popper in his right hand.

Hop was neither good looking nor clean-cut. He did not have an intelligent face. Drew ran with him because they grew up together, and though he was four years younger than Hop, he was already as strong as his older friend. Hop had eaten many dinners at his home, as many times as Drew could remember. His mother felt sorry for Hop, for the way he looked and acted, and for the way his family neglected him. She encouraged him to be a good young man. But he was not a good student, and he did not come from a good family. She had tried to provide her own son with as many advantages as possible in that part of Baltimore. But Hop was born with two strikes against him. He just did not have a chance at the plate, before he swung out for the third strike.

"Put the bag on the counter, mister," Hop said in a low voice as Drew stood frozen with the Coke in his hand, as the man beside him stood with the bag of cash.

"Pick it up," he said to Drew and pointed to it with the gun.

"What are you doin', man?" Drew said to him, pointing to the gun. "Put that thing down and let's get out of here," he said, but neither of them noticed that the man had pushed a button on the underside of the counter as he put the bag down.

"I ain't leavin' without the money, man," answered Hop. "I need the money."

"You never said nothin' about this, you can have my caddy money, take it, put that thing away. I'm not takin' the money," Drew said, "and we're gettin' out of here."

Drew moved away from the counter without taking the bag with the evening's receipts, and he left the side of the man who had secretly pushed the button.

Though he tried, he could not pull Hop out of the station before Hop grabbed the bag and they both ran.

It would be remembered later how things had happened. The Department of Social Services would take it into account. One would be saved and one was lost, but the saving was to come much later while the losing always happens much too quickly.

A squad car rounded the corner responding to the silent alarm that the station attendant had activated. Drew and Hop ran across Washington Boulevard to try to cross through the park and over the tracks which led through Mount Clare and then into Sandtown. But it was too late, and they would not get out of the park, they would not cross the tracks, not run through Mount Clare, and neither would Hop ever go into Sandtown again. It would not be for ten more years, until the year of our tennis matches, that the shaman priest's piece of clear crystal quartz would be found in the ground of the former plantation. And it did not protect the boys in the old plantation field that night, where it still lay buried in the ground undisturbed.

This was the story Drew told me that day after we had finished our tennis games. The Ivy League students had stopped to watch us play, and we were on our way for drafts and bluefish and mussels in the tavern by the university. After we finished our dinner, we left the tavern, and the beautiful dark-haired girl crossed the street. We were on our way to Diane's as he continued with his story.

The gas station man ran outside and yelled to the police as they skidded to a stop by the pumps and saw the two boys running across the road.

"He's got a gun; he's got a gun!"

They spun the car around and crossed the Boulevard sliding to a stop on the gravel of the parking lot on the other side. The boys had already crossed the lot and were running up the hill towards the old plantation house, as the first officer jumped out of the car, pulled his gun, and yelled to the boys to stop.

Drew grabbed his friend and Hop pushed him away, turning to face the police with the popper in his hand. Drew straightened up with his hands above his head. In the confusion, he heard a shot and Hop fell to the ground.

"It feels like my chest is burning inside."

Hop squeezed the words out of his mouth, lying on the ground trying to move. He was squirming on the grass. Drew looked down at him and saw a tiny hole in his shirt right over his heart. Hop was on the ground, face up, trying to move and he was squirming.

"My chest feels like it's burning inside."

Hop squeezed out the words again, his voice thick and heaving while he tried to move, and he was squirming on the grass.

"Then he stopped moving."

"He just looked up at me, and he died."

Drew tried to get Hop off the ground, and tried to keep his hands up high so the police could see. He tried to pick him up. He grabbed Hop's left arm but he could not lift him, and Hop fell back to the ground, the bag of money lay near his side. Drew bent over him one last time, his hand touched Hop's chest, and his finger went into the hole that the bullet had made. Then he saw the broken cylinder of the gun which lay beside

Hop's right hand. It had opened when he fell. There were no bullets in Hop's busted .22 caliber popper.

"Hello Darlings," Diane said later, when we reached her home and found her sitting on the terrace, drinking a glass of wine. At one time this was a very rich and prestigious neighborhood, not far from Center City.

Her only child was already in bed.

"Thanks for stopping by. You know how I hate to be alone in this house when John is away."

"Hello, Drew, so nice to see you again!"

She got up and kissed me. I put my arm around her and she leaned her weight against me.

"You're trembling," I said.

"Yes, I've had a frightfully awful day. You would not believe what I've gone through."

"Darling," she looked up at me.

"Please sit down, but first pour a glass of wine for yourself and for your friend."

15.
The Last Concert of Arthur Rubinstein

Arthur Rubinstein played his first American concert with the orchestra on January 8, 1906, three weeks shy of his nineteenth birthday at the Philadelphia Academy of Music. Tonight, seventy years later, on February 26, 1976, he would play his last concert there, at the age of 89. When he performed his first concert at the Academy on Broad Street in 1906, it was a long way from Piotrkowska Street in Lodz, Poland where he grew up. His last would be performed before an overflow audience and would end with a first-class overnight flight back to Paris.

The weather outside was cold that evening, but it was warm inside the doors of the Academy, with lines at each of the ticket windows filled with patrons who were fortunate enough to have purchased their tickets in advance. After receiving their tickets, they entered the lobby of the concert hall to deposit their coats and enter the old hall. The excitement of this final concert was tangible. You could feel and hear the energy and anticipation of what was to take place here this evening, seventy years after, and in the same place and on the same stage where the great pianist had made his debut with the orchestra so many years before.

There were five doors at the entrance of the concert hall on Broad Street, and I entered the second doorway, near the ticket booths on the left side of the entrance. It was not the first time I had heard Rubinstein play, but it would be my last. There would be no more concerts with as much con brio as that which would be heard here at the Academy this night.

I usually sat in the fourth-floor balcony when I attended concerts in this old hall, and would walk up the three flights on the steep wooden steps. The seats themselves were arranged steeply, in a shallow balcony, eight rows squeezed vertically to fit them into the space. Some seats had views partially obstructed by one or more of the fourteen columns that supported the fourth balcony and the three balconies below. I could not afford to care, and if the seats on the fourth floor were made of wood without padding, with seat backs so straight it was like sitting in a severe church pew, it did not matter. Some said the sound of the music here was the best in the hall. Never mind, perhaps a false concession made to those who could not afford the more expensive and comfortable seats on the lower balconies and the main floor below, upholstered places where I rarely sat.

I remembered one concert that Ricardo Muti conducted. Rudolf Serkin played Beethoven, and the tears flowed from the eyes of the woman who accompanied me that evening. I would find out later that she was a woman used to abuse, where she herself was the entertainment in the back seat of chauffeured limousines, driven by men who afforded protection to those seated in the back. When these men were through with her, they let her out of the car on the curb. They swung the door open from inside the car, so that she could exit alone onto the sidewalk outside the entrance to her apartment building. On that evening we sat together in our seats, house left, on the second-floor balcony circle, in one of the great musical venues of the world. I knew only that it was her first time in attendance for a concert in this place.

She was a fragile beauty who was expected at the end of any evening to remove all but the colored ribbon she usually wore around her throat. But she could still be overwhelmed by beauty, or perhaps when faced with it, unconsciously mourned the absence of it in her life. She was like a frightened, gentle child, afraid to do wrong for fear of punishment. She did not ask anything and expected nothing in return, except the expectation to entertain. Of all the privileged people in any audience I had seen, whether they were educated, elite, jeweled and polished, or the most humble, frequent, music lovers, none that I had ever seen were so moved by the music like this first-time concert mistress. The great master, the performance of whose concerto we had come to see and hear that evening, would have said that her blonde beauty belonged there on that evening, or on any other evening. She was one who had the least knowledge of the music being played, but perhaps through her suffering she was one who had the most innate understanding of why it had been created, and why it had to be performed.

But now at this winter's evening I was late – it had been a long day at the office – and the lines to the counter were moving slowly as Beethoven's Coriolanus Overture began. The Overture was played for the first time in 1807, in a private concert at the Prague Palace of the 7th Prince von Lobkowicz. The Piano Concerto No. 4 was played by Beethoven that evening for the first time as well. After that first performance, Beethoven's 4th Piano Concerto was performed by him again in 1808, in the first public performance in Vienna, and would not be performed again for twenty-eight years until 1836. That would be the last time Beethoven himself performed it, when his increasing deafness overtook his ability to play with an orchestra on a public keyboard.

The 4th G major Piano Concerto would be played again tonight by Rubinstein, here in Philadelphia, one hundred sixty-nine years after Beethoven's first performance in Prague in the palace of a prince.

Midway through the eight-minute overture I still stood at the counter to be told that none of the upper balcony seats were available, only main floor seating. The tension and drama of the music rose in me as I realized I did not have enough money to afford the more expensive seat. While the pleading questions and responses in the minor chords of the music built and overwhelmed the answers of the major keys, I had to withdraw from the window without a ticket, but I passed through the doors into the lobby, to stand and listen to the music.

The Coriolanus finished and applause rose and fell in the hall, and I knew that Rubinstein's great Steinway instrument was being moved to the front of the stage. Then silence again before the applause rose in a crescendo, and I knew that the great artist walked onto the stage from a door that opened on stage right.

A hush fell over the audience and the sound of a lone piano began to play upon the stage. Eugene Ormandy's baton brought the musicians to life and the orchestra repeated the theme begun by the piano, now in a rising key, and I knew that I had to leave.

I exited the doors to the street outside of the Academy, the memory of a Rubinstein recording of Beethoven's 4th Concerto continued to play on in my mind. By the time I reached home to my apartment, I knew that the intermission would be over and that Rubinstein would have begun playing the Brahms Piano Concerto No. 1 without me.

16.
The Migrants

You had to get off the main highway, away from all the traffic, to get to Erdesville. It was a one stoplight town, down a long lazy slope from the main highway because it was bottom land, beyond where the source of the Tuscarawas River began at the old Indian portage trail. The Indians once carried their canoes across the divide here to the Cuyahoga, which flows north to the Erie Great Lake. The Tuscarawas River flows south, meandering on its way through Ohio's glaciated hills until it joins the Ohio River which flows to the Mississippi River, where it finally spreads out and slows on its way through the Louisiana delta and out into the Gulf of Mexico.

There were still traces of the old canal that followed the river south, but these were overgrown and now largely forgotten, not yet turned into newly awakened towpath trails to be used once again, for a new kind of recreational commerce.

The reason for the existence of this town was the black soil of the surrounding farms, muck farms, Ralph called them. From these lowlands which were hot and humid in the summertime, you lived with the risk and the promise of fertile flooding, and the certainty of swarms of mosquitos. Wealthy landowners owned the farms to which oil company men delivered fuel. It was my job to sand and paint the farm tanks which stood at the edges of the fields, steel tanks which held the fuel for all the agricultural machinery used to work the farms. It was dirty, sweltering work. You had to brush and scrape the tanks before they were painted, and the rust flakes fell into your eyes and burned even though you tried to protect them with the cheap goggles you wore. You had to crawl over and under the tanks with a wire brush and scrape the rust off of them from top to bottom. The rust fell like rain from the horizontal cylindrical shapes of the three-hundred-gallon tanks, and you were in the midst of it without an umbrella.

The bib lettuce season always excited Ralph, who was one of the drivers at the oil company which serviced these farms. He always knew when the lettuce was ready to be picked and he would bring back baskets of it to take home and to share with the men at the shop.

"Oooh-wee," he would exclaim when he brought a basket of new bib lettuce into the office.

Slick, one of the other drivers, only talked and criticized the workers in the fields with lewd comments about the Mexican women.

At the end of each day, we gathered in the small oil company office, to sit and rest for a few minutes and talk about the schedule for the next day before we all headed home. When Ralph came into the office, he would go to the refrigerator, pull the lever, open the door, and throw a dime into the tin cup. He would take out a coke, pop off the cap, sit down on one of the chairs beside the two desks which faced each other – one for the owner and one for the office manager – take a long sip from the bottle, and begin to talk using his hands as well as his words.

He shook out the fingers of his left hand loosely, holding the Coke in his right hand.

"Oooh-wee, the bib lettuce sure looks good this year!"

That's when Slick would begin to talk about the girls who worked in the fields, with descriptions that came out of the hills where he was born and raised. He had a way of speaking using vulgar profanity which I had never heard before, not even from the novel *Tropic of Cancer*, which I was reading for the first time that summer, and not even from the tables of the all-night card games which I would experience later that fall at the university.

Trucks rolled into our oil company past the small office all through the summer. Five-thousand-gallon tanks, one with road oil, the other with sweet smelling and plasticky RS2, lay on their sides beyond the driveway facing the office. A loading platform was built between the two tanks eight feet above the ground accessed by an iron ladder fixed to the wooden platform. A dispensing pump for diesel fuel sat on the top of the platform. The road oil in the first tank was for dust control, the second tank held the rapid-setting bituminous emulsion RS2 tar which was used for chip-and-seal country roads.

To maintain these less traveled county roads, a thick layer of the RS2 is sprayed onto the road upon which fine limestone gravel is layered on top, both of which congeal together into a durable smooth surface after countless cars and trucks pass over it. The stones glue in place, and by the end of a long, hot summer, the clouds of limestone dust kicked up by the cars and trucks have settled down and helped seal the surface of the road.

The men who drove the trucks were hard, no-nonsense men. They were outwardly kind only if you needed help, and then they were even solicitous. They were skilled drivers who settled into their old truck seats and became part of the apparatus that spewed oil onto the county roads. During work hours they were tools useful only at the wheel. They gave you a hard time while you loaded their trucks until they decided that you were not a complete idiot. But they assumed you were one until they got to know you. They gave you a hard time because they knew you were going to the university at the end of the summer. They had not gone to college, some had not graduated from high school, and they did not think you knew how to survive outside of a classroom. There was no resentment to your going to college, unless you acted like you knew that they had not. In fact, they respected your education plans once they got to know you, and told you to get an education or you would have to work the way that they had to work. They freely gave you this advice once they believed you knew how to work hard, and that you could work without complaint.

These men could maneuver a truck into a narrow space with an incongruous delicacy, using only their mirrors and language best left on the roads. If you got in their way, they let you know with a shout and a curse. It was hot, heavy work, and they breathed the dust and the fumes each day of the summer, for weeks and months on end until the autumn came.

There was no air-conditioning in the trucks in those days, and after they pulled up to the tanks they would climb out of the cabs and go directly into the tiny air-conditioned office to sit a spell as I loaded their trucks. They pulled the bottles out of the old fridge, threw in their dimes, and pried the caps off to drink a Coke or a Nehi soda in that small, cool space. Everyone smoked, and the air inside turned blue when the drivers were in the office. When the owner was in the office, cigar smoke also filled the air. Since you could not smoke outside on the grounds of the oil company, it was only inside the small office where you could smoke. We were surrounded by combustible tanks of gasoline, kerosene, fuel oil, road oils and tar, which baked all day long in the hot and humid summer sun.

As soon as a truck pulled up to the loading tanks, the office manager opened the door and yelled out the loading instructions to me. If it were a road oil run, I was told how many gallons of kerosene I had to add to the oil when I filled the truck. For a chip and seal job, the RS2 went straight from the storage tank into the truck tank. Loading the road oil and RS2 trucks was my responsibility when I was not out in the field painting the three-hundred-gallon farm tanks.

There was an old filling station in Erdesville which had not been painted for years. It was a station that was owned by our company, and it was one of my jobs that summer to paint it inside and out. No one remembered how long it had been since it had seen a fresh coat of paint. The white paint on the outside walls of concrete blocks had faded and blistered and turned gray, and was discolored where weeds and small tree saplings had grown up against it on the sides and the back of the station. The concrete block walls were exposed up to the first eight or nine courses, then corrugated metal siding which did not need to be painted rose all the way to the triangle of the pitch of the roof. In the front of the station, facing it from the road, the office was to the right, with two service bays on the left. The inside walls of the service bays needed to be painted all the way to the ceiling. I did not have to paint the inside of the office. One of the office walls was covered with a calendar and a cork bulletin board filled with pictures thumbtacked to the cork. The other wall was covered by a bookcase behind the desk. The bookcase was filled with parts and repair manuals, and covered the entire wall so that the wall itself was no longer visible.

All through the summer, trucks rumbled past the Erdesville station, going to and from the fields. In the morning, the road was filled with flatbed trucks carrying migrant workers to the fields. During the day, a steady stream of produce exited the town in trucks weighed down with their fresh, moisture laden cargo come from the fields. Finally, at the end of the day, flatbed trucks with wooden slats fitted on the sides for hand holds, returned the migrant workers back to the camps.

Each morning before I drove to Erdesville I loaded my flatbed truck with ladders and paint cans, brushes, rollers and handles, rags and tarps, scrapers and wire brushes. The lunch pail and thermos I took with me in the cab. I remember stretching out on the top rungs of the ladder inside the station, where the wall rose to the top of the triangle it made as it met the peak of the roof. I balanced paint cans and paint brushes, and reached out farther than I should have each time before I moved the ladder to an unpainted area. The cans of paint swung like church bells from hooks which fastened them to the rungs of the ladder. The cans had to be carried down each time I moved the ladder, and carried back up to the spot where I continued my work. They needed to be rehung again and again on the rungs of the ladder, each time I moved it to an unpainted section.

It was summer work for me, and the mechanics in the station tolerated my presence. I was as seasonal as the workers carried to the fields, so I worked as quietly and efficiently as I could, trying to earn not their respect, but my own. I was not important enough for them to care about me. I might be around for a summer or two, but then I would graduate and go away, and not come back again. There was no reason for them to invest any energy in me as long as I did my job.

I remember the smell of the oils, gasoline, and diesel fuel; the sunburned faces of truck drivers, the burning in my eyes from the rust flakes when I scraped a rusty tank. From time-to-time Slick's West Virginia blessings are reminded back to me, along with the smell of tobacco in the office, Ralph's hands, and his baskets full of bib lettuce.

I remember one day when I sat on top of a couple of paint cans, and leaned back up against the front of the Erdesville station. I was young, and tall, and strong then, wearing workman's clothing splashed with paint, eating a sandwich my mother prepared for me out of my lunch bucket. A flatbed truck drove by on its way to the fields. It carried ten or twelve young Mexican women standing in the back of the truck holding onto the wooden sides. The lettuce pickers saw me as they passed by the station, they were singing something and laughing. As they passed by me, they all turned towards me and waved and sang and smiled, as the motion of the truck caused them to sway from side to side, as they rounded the corner by the station. They moved with the motion of the truck as if in rhythm to their song. They were all singing together, waving, and I waved to them in return; and turning back away from me, they headed out of town into the fields.

17.
There is Something I Want to Tell You

The dead Sergeant's younger brother had been very wrong, when he wrote home from London in November 1942, that the war would soon be over.

On the afternoon of 13January1945 the older brother went down by the bank of the river to get some straw to make a bed at the bottom his foxhole. The platoons from Company I, 75th Infantry Division, 291st Regiment were already dug-in near the river. The German shelling was constant since they had arrived at Manhay at the end of December. The 3rd Platoon had just gone down to get rations and when they returned, a shell exploded and a piece of shrapnel entered his stomach, a very small piece, perhaps as big as a dime, but it hit a vital spot and caused internal bleeding. They laid him on the straw, and opened up his great coat to try to find the wound to stop the bleeding, before the medic ran over to take control.

"Stay with me!" the medic cried as he tried to find the artery which was puddling blood inside the heavy wool greatcoat

"I've got you now, Sergeant, stay with me!" he ordered.

"What's the name of your wife, what's her name!" he shouted, seeing the ring on his left hand, but he tried and could not find the source of the bleeding, and he could not stop it.

"Stay with me! Stay with me!"

There was nothing more anyone could do to save the life of the staff sergeant. He lasted a very short time before he bled to death. One of his buddies, a 1st Lieutenant from 2nd platoon, was four hundred yards away when he heard about it, but before he got there to see his friend, he was already dead. The sergeant was just one of the men who were lost there by the bank of the Salm River at Grand Halleux, in January 1945.

Four months after he died, the sergeant's young widow received a letter from the Lieutenant who had been her husband's friend. He was taking liberties with censorship regulations that forbade the mentioning of casualties in combat.

"Men sometimes write things that they think they saw, and cause unnecessary heartaches," the Lieutenant wrote.

That was why her only letter of notification had come from the Regimental Commander, not even from the chaplain.

It was the Lieutenant who told her what had happened on the day that her husband was killed. He told her that her husband would not want her to let the bottom drop out of all her plans and ideas. He told her that she needed to go on and live her life with the certainty of his loss. He told her that the men in her husband's 3rd platoon, cried that January afternoon when he died. The young widow cried with this letter in May, now with the certain knowledge that her husband would not come home. She read the letter in the springtime back home, how the men had wept on the cold and snow-covered Flemish field in January. That was just the kind of guy her husband was, his friend the Lieutenant wrote, and now she knew with a final acknowledgement, that her husband would never come home.

Both of the brothers were sergeants, and by chance they were both in Great Britain at the end of November 1944. The younger was in London, while the older trained in Wales after arriving on a ship that left New York on November 14, after eighteen months of training, first at the Louisiana Maneuver Area at Camp Breckenridge, Kentucky, and then at Fort Leonard Wood, Missouri. The older brother was in the infantry, his younger brother in an army intelligence Signal Radio Company. English was not the mother tongue for either of these soldiers of immigrant parents, and both of the brother's spoke

German. It was the younger brother's job to listen in his headphones from London for German intercepts, while orders sent the older one across the channel in December 1944 to land in France, first at the port of Le Havre, then on to Rouen on December 13, and to bivouac at Yvetot on December 14. From there, the 291st Regiment of the 75th Infantry Division moved two hundred fifty miles east, and arrived at Tongres, Belgium, on Dec 22.

Both of the brothers were good athletes, and the older was a born leader. The younger rode a motorcycle, the older rode a horse, boarding his Tennessee Walker in a neighbor's barn. Both had many friends, and hunted and fished in the hills and the rivers near their home, and collected fruit in late summer from a neighbor's orchard, which their mother and sisters canned for weeks in order to put up the fruit for winter. The older brother built a secret cabin on a neighbor's land in the woods, for a club with his friends who had names like Toad, Red, Fritz, and Smitty. He would be the first to marry, and the first to go to war. He owned a little country store with a bar and beer tap in the back, and it was to his younger brother that the business came to be taken care of until he too, went to war when he came of age. So, it seemed that all his life, the younger brother followed the older one.

The older brother's regiment in Belgium was in reserve for four days to rest in the snow and the cold at Tongres before they moved up to the front at Manhay on the 27th, two days after Christmas in 1944. They had another two days of rest at the beginning of the second week of January 1945, before they relieved the 82nd Airborne Division in the fight at Grand Halleux, along the Salm River.

A few days after his friend died there, the Lieutenant also got hit, but he survived. He was from Minnesota, a land of wide-open spaces. The older brother had planned to move there after the war, to forget what he had seen, and to start life all over. The Lieutenant told him it was a place for horses and farms, a good place for his Tennessee Walker, far from either coast and the oceans that led east or west, as far from the places where the violence had been, as it was possible for anyone to go.

It would be a long journey home for the older brother, from his death in January 1945 to October 1947, when with 6,248 men killed-in-action, the dead sergeant returned to the port of New York aboard the Liberty ship Joseph V. Connolly. It was almost three years to the day since he had left for England. The coffin of one soldier was chosen, and taken from the hold of the ship to be the Unknown, a soldier from the Battle of the Bulge, placed on a horse drawn caisson, and rolled down the brick and steel canyon of Fifth Avenue to Central Park. It rolled through the city streets amidst a crowd of one million grateful mourners. The only sound was the muffled drums of the honor guard, and the horse's hooves upon the street.

By November 1944 both brothers had known that the war would soon be over. The older brother sent a Christmas message from Belgium and said he wanted to meet in England and talk things over before they both shipped back home. For the rest of his life the younger brother wanted to know what it was his older brother wished to say to him at the end of the war. Fifty years later he would sit at my dinner table to tell me with a visceral anguish, that he was still waiting to find out what it was his brother had wanted to talk to him about.

He would never understand that all it was, was a way for the older to say goodbye, to say he was not coming home to the family, or to his store, or to the places in which they had grown up. He was going to be the first one, and the only one, to leave home and the family again, to try to begin a new life in a new place, with his wife and his Lieutenant friend, who would help him try to forget the things that he saw, in the short two months before he died.

18.
The Killings

All night long on the flight from Atlanta, I watched the storm clouds rise in the distance. The pilots flew wide of the huge thunderheads that towered high above the altitude of the plane, visible outside of the cabin windows in the sky around us. Lightning flashed within the rising cloud formations forty-five thousand feet above the ground, like great flickering lamps whose filaments burned out when the heat and the light of the storm consumed them. I sat in my window seat and looked out over the Great Plains unseen below in the night, and wondered if this time tornadoes would touch down in the part of Oklahoma that we were flying towards. I wondered if we would be able land and if I would finally be able to collapse into bed, after another long flight at the end of another long day, repeated two or three times a week. There was never enough sleep to escape from the fatigue and stress of a six-days-a-week, twelve-hours-a-day work schedule that often required seven days of work and two or three cross-country flights each week in addition to the time spent in my two offices. I was captured midway between the east coast and the Great Plains. It was a schedule that tried to break you down to see if you were good enough to get to the next executive level. I watched the beauty of the violence in the distance, safe in my cabin seat, wondering if we could land or if storm generated winds would push us away to another place to which I did not want to go. It would only mean an enforced break in my schedule, that would make things even more difficult when I finally got back to my offices.

The girl in the room next to mine was having a time of it with the man who had hired her, waking me from a deep sleep with the noise they made when the headboard of their bed banged against the eggshell of a wall that separated us. I would not stay here again, in this cheap, company approved hotel. With the hours I worked and the flights back and forth across the country I could not afford to have my sleep dwarfed in the few hours I had to myself each day. She was young and I could hear her say that she had not yet tired of the work, or of the middle-aged doctor with whom she was with before they had fulfilled the contract between them. He sounded more like an uneducated worker than a professional man, as he called out to her and pleaded to let him satisfy her.

"Most of the men I am with are so plastic," I heard her say to the doctor as she began to work on him.

"They are so fake, and their lives are so empty, they have nothing to say. I'm only nineteen years old, but I am interesting, and I like to talk about things when I am with someone, and not just do it with them without talking."

"Come here, honey," the doctor replied, "You know I'm not like the others."

She wanted to talk, and he was willing to listen to her, to a point.

"You are interesting, and I like talking to you, and it's not just the money that you need, I can tell. You still want to know if it means more to me than just this one thing, and if I care about you when we are together, and not just for this."

They knew one another. This one had a regular schedule with her. After all the noise and the talking I heard the door open and close from their room. I could hear the skipping sounds of an excited, happy girl as her shadow passed by the thin covering of my room's only window. She was skipping on the sidewalk on her way to the soda machine by the side of the office, which was at the end of the walkway that led to the doors of our adjoining rooms.

I was so tired I could not stay awake in spite of the noise, but before I fell asleep again, her breath quickened loudly, and she said something to the man who was with her.

"You are not like the others," she said over and over and over again, "you are not like all the others," she repeated again and again and again, until she cried out and finally satisfied, both herself and him.

I always ate alone at night, in whatever restaurant I found after leaving the office on the way to my hotel. But tonight, the public auditor with whom I was working had invited me to his house for dinner with him and his wife. He was not much older than me, but was already married with a home and a professional career. He produced beautiful work papers at the office. I was to find out that evening that he wanted to become a business owner. His life's goal was to own a major roller coaster theme park. He loved roller coasters, and was knowledgeable about all of the best of them across the country, especially the old and historic wooden ones, the kinds that made you nostalgic for a simpler past, or at least the past that you thought was simpler. These were the rides which were not designed using computer programs. These were rides from a time of more modest expectations. It required the thrill of holding hands and sitting close together with your date, to complete the human interaction with the ride. It was not an experience of man versus machine, and a terrifying singular excitement. It was personal. Human. Heart to heart.

He was way ahead of me in the life planning department. Compared to him, my life was a patchwork of randomly occurring events. I had no doubt that I would someday read about him in the financial pages.

The following day my work took me to Dallas. That evening I sat at a table in a new restaurant recommended to me by one of my colleagues at work. It was late, I was alone in the dining room. All of the patrons had already eaten and left, and I was there for the last hour of the evening. I ordered, and as I sat waiting for my dinner, drinking a cup of coffee, another man entered, looked around at all the empty tables, and asked if he could join me. He said he did not like to eat alone, if I did not mind. Happy for the company, he sat down across from me at my table set for four.

He was very much less than six-foot tall, already in the process of becoming overweight, with thinning hair and a pale complexion. He was middle-aged, at least twenty years older than me, and said he was working in the area on some kind of research for a project he did not specify. He wore a light-colored suit, round metal-framed glasses, and looked through the lenses with pale tired eyes. He had a careworn look about him, and an unhealthy pallor. The strangest thing about him was his voice, higher pitched than average, and quite nasal. He was not the kind of man a woman would find physically attractive.

He ordered a drink against my coffee, and the waiter came back for his dinner request, in time so that his dinner could be brought out together to the table with mine. At least I would not have to eat in front of this stranger, as he waited for his own order to be prepared. We exchanged pleasantries, and I leaned forward on the table, my coffee cup at my right hand, and my left on the table, politely feigning interest. He leaned into the table and slowly and without hesitation began to talk, just as the waitress returned through the kitchen door with our dinners.

The Kennedy assassination had been in the news again lately, with reports and final government conclusions, and he asked me if I had been keeping up with the news. He said the truth may never be known, and that a lot of the information was to remain sealed from public access for fifty years. Then he said he worked for the government and was going to tell me about the Kennedy assassination, reached for his glass to take a sip of this drink, and continued to talk.

"The Warren Report got it all wrong, and they knew it," he said to me.

"They had to present the big lie. Oswald didn't act alone, it was the Cubans, and Castro, and the Russians who had Kennedy killed, because he and Bobby tried to take Castro down, and humiliate Khrushchev. It was enough, after the Powers affair. It was a warning when they killed his girlfriend, the actress."

"Others were involved too, that's where the money came into it, and all of this is too much for the public to know and to handle. The government can't admit what happened, can't admit the revenge that came back to us here after the amateur hour disaster that was the Bay of Pigs, and after we allowed the goddamned missiles to come so close."

"Maybe someday a long time from now, we will all know what really happened in Dallas, Havana, and in Moscow, though the Russians were too smart to get involved with a direct link to Oswald. When they expelled him, they let him take his Russian wife with him, nothing else."

"When a man learns to speak Russian while he is still in the US military, is court-marshalled from the army, goes to Russia and gets married, tries to go to Cuba via Mexico City, denounces the US and tries to revoke his citizenship, kills the president, and in turn is murdered by a Dallas night club operator with questionable business associates, well, there are just too many coincidences to let you believe that the man acted alone, and not under the direction of an enemy agent. It is just a too improbably perfect story."

At the end of this discussion, he reached over and put his right hand on top of my left. I removed my hand from under his and ignored the gesture.

"A CIA story."

I did not know whether or not to believe a word of what he had just told me, but I kept listening with a perverse fascination to this stranger, with his high-pitched nasal voice, colorless eyes, metal rimmed glasses, and small hands that now moved in front of him, and around him, and flitted over his plate, and about his face like birds, as he talked.

Two nights before, a very young prostitute and a middle-aged doctor had disturbed my sleep, Last night I enjoyed the wholesome normalcy of a young husband and wife, who planned their lives and dreams together. Tonight, the pale middle-aged man who almost dined alone, instead sat and talked to me, a stranger at a table of a randomly chosen restaurant.

I remained in my seat and finished my last cup of coffee, but in my mind, I had already exited the dining room. As I withdrew, I imagined the man with thin, colorless hair, talking to a younger listener, me, now removed. I withdrew far enough, and could see but could not hear, as he motioned with his hands, illuminated with the light above the table which reflected off his glasses. His hands told the story about the humiliation of a country, the revenge against another, the death of an actress and of a president, and the betrayal and death of the criminals who had agreed to bring it all about. All the while, the amplified sound of steel wheels rolling on tracks bolted to a wooden structure, drowned out the sounds of a man and woman in the room next door.

19.
The Writer

She was walking behind us and she heard us talking before we sat down on the park bench by the side of the path. She asked us if we were Americans, and did we mind if she sat on the bench with us.

"We are Russian and American," I laughed as we invited her to sit down with us.

"Moscow and New York, bitte setzen sie sich. Wir wohnen beide hier."

"We both live here."

She spoke a few words in English, then resumed her German as we all switched languages to her own. She sat down heavily on the park bench beside us. She asked if we minded if she smoked. There were two remaining cigarettes and a cheap plastic lighter in the cardboard pack of the Gauloises that she held. You could buy two of the lighters for one euro, anywhere they sold cigarettes.

"Someone gave me this lighter as a gift," she affirmed.

She took off her glasses and laid them on her lap, took out one of the cigarettes with swollen nicotine-stained fingers and unkempt nails, and put the cigarette between her lips. She rolled the wheel against the flint three times before it lit, then bent over with difficulty to touch the end of the cigarette to the flame of the lighter. Her hair almost touched the flame as it fell down across her forehead. The tobacco at the end of the cigarette began to burn, and her head sprang back away from the flame as she uncoiled her back and lowered the extinguished lighter in her left hand. She inhaled deeply with a long drag on the cigarette, and breathed out the smoke with a sigh. She put the lighter into the pack with the one remaining cigarette and picked up her eyeglasses with her left hand, lenses spotted and dusty from the fingerprints and flakes from the dry skin of her face and from her thinning hair. The eyeglass frame was bent on the left side, and with her right hand holding the cigarette, fit them onto her face with a toggled back and forth motion, and looked up and out over the park with the protruding eyes of one who has an overactive thyroid. Her lungs were congested and she coughed and tried to clear them without any effect as she adjusted her seat on the bench.

She began to chat in the way one does who does not have someone to talk to each day, and though she seemed a bit odd and spoke a bit slowly it was apparent that she was an intelligent, educated person. But she spoke as aimlessly as if she had memorized a stream of consciousness script, and was no longer aware of, nor cared about, what she was saying.

She looked out over the green space in front of us, surrounded on one side by the open Stadtgraben rivulet, just one of many small streams which flowed out from one of the many city canals, and behind it the ancient city wall, still extant. From here the rivulet split north to form the InnerCity canal, where it still turned an ancient water wheel at the Avian Gate of the fortress wall, and then partially diverted east to form the Outside City canal.

"You can't really sit or sleep on the lawn here, there is too much waste on the grass from the dogs," she offered.

"I feel sad," she continued after a pause on this sunny, late autumn day, "because I did not sleep well. Then I got up and started smoking."

"The people who clean my flat on the weekends were not able to come this morning. I am not able to do it myself anymore. I have diabetes, and my friend also has diabetes and has to use a wheelchair. My daughter has diabetes worse than mine, because she's had it since she was a child."

A man, not quite middle-aged, stopped in front of us.

"Have you seen a light brown shepherd dog, about this high?" he said.

He indicated a dog that came up to just above his knee, and he was holding a thick leather leash. He looked as if he was about to begin to cry.

"Sorry," we said, "we have not seen it."

He hurried away, approaching all the other people on the walking path of the park, each of whom shook their heads, until soon he was out of sight. A few minutes later we saw a medium size light brown dog with some people at the other end of the lawn. We could not tell if the dog belonged to them or not, but when they left the end of the park, the dog went with them. It did not look like a shepherd.

"I like cats. But I am afraid of the large black breed of dogs, Dobermans."

"She also likes cats," I smiled, nodding to my companion.

"I like dogs," I added.

"I have a cousin who lives in Los Angeles. I only visited her once. America is a very large country. I was born in Stuttgart, and it was very difficult after the war when I was a little girl. When I was old enough to remember things, most of the rubble had been cleared, but the remaining factories were still being emptied of equipment. We were not allowed to rebuild the factories for two more years. I only understood this later when I was able to write about it."

"We were told to become farmers, that we had to be humbled and to experience hunger because of the war. That is why the vineyards and weekend house gardens that surround Stuttgart to the southeast are planted on the hills that rise to the city above the main railway line. They are planted all the way to the edge of the city. After the Morgenthau directive was lifted, we rebuilt the factories very quickly, although it was almost a year after the speech of hope in Stuttgart before we were allowed to rebuild."

"I do not see my sister very often. It is two hundred kilometers from Stuttgart to Munich where my daughter and my sister live, but now I live here. It is only sixty kilometers to Munich, but I still don't see them very often."

"Everyone has a mobile phone," she said, looking at mine. "I think I should get a handy, too. I'm very unhappy with the phone company. I want to cancel my phone. They call me when I am in bed to offer me something. I think it is a friend or my daughter calling and I get happy, but it is not them, just the phone company, and I am disappointed."

"I was supposed to get married twice. I was engaged once, but it did not work out. The second time, after my daughter was born, he just left."

She pointed to my pants.

"Jeans are very modern. I also have jeans, but today I took out my jogging pants."

"I was a writer by profession. Maybe I should have become a journalist. But maybe by now I would be dead because I could have been sent somewhere dangerous and got killed. I don't like the local Allgemeine newspaper anymore because it has become too right-wing."

We sat for a few more moments in silence. The afternoon was getting on and we still wanted to walk back through the entertainment of the Zentrum.

"It was very nice to meet you, and to be able to talk with you this afternoon," I said as we both got up.

"When I woke up this morning, I did not know I would meet such a nice couple, and that it would be so pleasant to talk. It was very nice for me, too. Vielen Dank!" she said.

"Have a beautiful afternoon."

We walked to the end of the park from where we had been sitting, and climbed the steps of the old city wall behind the open-air theater on Red Gate Strasse. When we looked back towards the bench where we had all sat together, we were surprised that she was already gone. We could not see her anywhere on the path in the distance, for as far as we could see.

20.
Russian Soldiers

If you walked down the Avenue to circle the Centrum on the körút, crossed the Oktogon, and continued on from bridge to bridge in a half circle from the river, you would pass Russian soldiers, off-duty, who were still to be seen on the street. The Budapesti búcsú – Budapest Farewell – would not yet be celebrated for another year until June 1991, the day the Russians would leave the country. Now they walked in pairs, uniforms the only clothes they possessed, and no one greeted them or looked at them when they passed. They were not welcomed here in the city, off of their military bases. The green of their uniforms was as drab as the clothes worn by all of the other passersby. There would be no color on the streets for at least another year or two.

Some of them were just kids, with caps worn at comical angles it seemed to western eyes, and the youngest ones walked with the careless loose gait and sloping shoulders of those unconcerned with uncertain futures and less hope. Their Russian conversations never paused when we walked by, and they ignored us as much as we ignored them. They were accustomed to being tolerated by the older citizens, and discretely ridiculed by the younger, bolder sons and daughters, now the grandsons and granddaughters of those whom had survived the war and then the failed revolution.

Both sides considered this attitude a large step forward from earlier times, though the Russians knew their time was running out. The people of this city knew that the Russian time was over. Many in this once again liberated country believed that the soldiers preferred life here, even a life of relative deprivation and limitation, to the one that awaited them back home in one of the eleven times zones of their far-flung country. Theirs was a country also in the midst of an historic upheaval, and all there who remembered or experienced the blood of the twentieth century hoped that this transition to a new country and a new century would be a less bloody one.

By June 19, 1991 the forty thousand remaining Russian soldiers would leave the country by command of Colonel General Burlakov and Lieutenant General Silov. They would exit from almost six thousand buildings in seventy army camps and air bases, and a Russian request which would remain unmet for billions in reparations for the buildings and equipment which were abandoned and left behind on the "Farewell Day."

You could take in much of the history of this threadbare city whose geographic beauty had never faded – from the ancient ruins of a cloister on Margit Sziget, from the bullet pockmarked walls left by the Arrow Cross executions, the medieval domed octagonal thermal baths built by the conquering Ottoman Turks, or the Aquincum Roman ruins which jutted out of the median strip between the lanes of the road which leads north out of the city to the artist village of Szendendre. Decades of neglect seemed to cover everything in a wash of grays, and blacks, and muted whites. The people were as colorless as the expressions on their faces. There was a sense of resignation in a shopkeeper's indifference, or in the comment of a hotel concierge.

"Why would you want to live here?"

"Life is hard."

Exhaust fumes of oil and gasoline and diesel fuel spewed from the vehicles on the street. The diesel smoke from truck engines designed five decades earlier before the war, helped to make the air so thick you could not see to the other side of the Danube when you stopped at a table by the river for a coffee, beer, or a glass of pálinka. A headache followed if you lingered too long or too near to the traffic. The waiters in those cafes would take advantage of anyone who did not speak the language. Overcharges were as exorbitant as the spinning meters of the notorious bandit taxis that waited on the streets for their next victim.

Still, by the time spring came in that first year after the wall fell, the lilacs reappeared, and if an old woman struggled to push open a three-meter-tall ancient wooden door to the courtyard of her building, there might be branches of the blossoms in her hand or in her basket. The emotions of love and innocence expressed in the purple and white flowers were in evidence everywhere. On the days when the sun poked through the pollution and disappointment, the beauty of the unmarried young women celebrated the return of the warmth and the hope of a new year, and the young men stood on the bridges to watch them sunbathe their bare breasts on the bank of the Danube below. From the top of Hármashatárhegy, Three Border Mountain, young people gathered on summer nights around fires to celebrate a szalonnasütés, to cook the fatted pork and let the fat drip onto pieces of bread. The view remained breathtakingly beautiful of the Danube flowing beneath the seven bridges spanning the river, which divided Buda from Pest.

We did not know enough to keep our garage door closed to the street, or the gate through which you had to pass before you entered the driveway with the grass growing between the open spaces of the concrete blocks which were sunk into the soil. The garage door opened to the cars, the bicycles, the two storage rooms, and the door into which you entered the lower level of our house. We did not know that everyone kept their front entrance gate closed and locked to the walkway that led to the front door, or that the bicycles ought not to be left on the grass of the front garden until night when they were put away, and only then the garage door and gate locked and closed. Our yard and home was as open as it was from the place from which we had come. The iron fences around the yard and the front gate served only as a backdrop to the perennially blooming portulacas, which we planted with seeds brought from home. We did not think of the fences as keeping in or out.

Later, after our neighbors became acquainted with us, they told us it was not safe to leave everything so open, though they liked to see the children playing in the garden, and riding their bikes on the utca, or going to the rocky park that lay at the end of the street with its hilly paths, park benches, small cave, and a view of the five-hundred-twenty-eight meter mountain, János-hegy, with its cable lift to the Erzsébet kilátó in the distance. The cable lift took you from the base of the mountain, which lay just beyond the residence of the American ambassador, to the top for the skiers and hikers who chose not to drive up on the road from the other side of the mountain.

There was rarely any personal crime here in the city, young women could safely jog through the neighborhoods alone at any hour of the day, but theft could occur if you did not take care. A car window might be smashed if anything of value was left in open view if you went into the city. But none of this ever happened in our neighborhood.

Red currants grew along the fence behind our home, where the widow lived with her daughter. She was a kindly old woman, with patience for the children if a ball went over the fence into her yard. Then they would need to exit our garden through the front gate and go around the corner to the next street which ended in a staircase of stone steps which took it to the street below. The widow's home was the last at the top of the hill before the steps, behind our home, and they had to ring the bell at her gate. If she saw them, she knew that they had come for a ball in her yard, and there was no irritation in her for the needs of a well-mannered child. It was she who asked them if they liked to eat the currants which grew on either side of our shared fence, both on her side and on ours, and she showed them how to mix them with cream, and make a simple treat. It was the only time we had any contact with her, as she, like all the others, lived behind a closed gate and an iron fence.

A long time ago. The widow long dead, and her daughter now middle-aged. The home which had not been touched since the war has now since been refurbished and become a jewel on this hill in District II. Now there is a beautiful re-planted garden, a hand-wrought stainless-steel gate, and privacy hedges against the fence where once the red currants grew, which my children mixed with cream, when our gates were still left open.

From time to time, I pause and lift the handle from the closet shelf where it lies, release the lock from the scabbard, and pull the knife blade free. It is still sharp as a razor, the locking mechanism and blade clean and uncorroded. It would still slide and lock onto the end of a gun barrel as cleanly as it did thirty years ago, when it fit onto the end of the Russian assault rifle for which it was made.

The two soldiers had entered our open gate together, come to the door to politely ask if we would buy anything from them, in that year before they left our city to go back home. They were polite, and could speak English well enough to show us and tell us what they had to sell which we might want to buy. A Lenin pin, a Red Star pin, a Young Pioneer scarf, and the bayonet for me. It was not easy for them to approach strangers in this country where they were not welcomed, but need makes action if you want to survive. They were polite, gentle young men, fond of children, and they smiled at the sight of the bicycles and balls in the garden.

I replace the handle on the closet shelf as I pause to think of them, and the world that had not yet changed, in that time before we learned to lock our gates.

21.
Harold T. Clark Courts

I opened another beer and he lit another cigarette. There were now five empty bottles in front of me on my side of the table, and an ashtray was filling up on his side. He took a deep drag on the cigarette, turned his face away from me, and exhaled.

"I don't know why, I never really loved her, but she wanted to get married."

He changed the subject.

"He lives on the other side of the water, over there."

The Caloosahatchee River lay between.

"I don't think he'll ever be the same," he continued, "he had a great marriage, beautiful children, really let his friends down, especially the ones who introduced them."

"He still has a pretty fucking big house over there. I don't feel sorry for him, it's just one of his houses. And he's got a big fucking boat over there somewhere, too. I'd like to be him for just one fucking day!"

"How could you marry her if you didn't love her? You were with her a long time."

"She wanted to get married, so I told her we could. I didn't really care one way or another. I didn't think about it. She kept asking and it was after we had lived together for five years. She said she loved me anyway."

"Woody said you wouldn't come out of the house, that he had to come and get you. Everyone was waiting in the back yard to begin the ceremony and we didn't understand why you wouldn't come out. She was the only one who didn't seem to be worried about it."

"She knew how I was and she understood."

Woody said later that she really was the only one who understood me. She knew I didn't want to get married. She knew I was just doing it because she wanted it, because we had already been together for so many years.

"If you didn't want to marry her, why did you do it?" he asked.

I ignored the repeated question as long as I could.

"She wanted to have children, that's when we had to split. She said she couldn't wait anymore. I didn't really care. It was still friendly between us, she didn't hate me, but she was disappointed. She knew I never loved her. We went in front of the judge and signed the papers. There was no arguing or discussion. I know it bothered her about the children thing, but she knew I couldn't do it."

"I'm still wearing this ring."

It was since high school, a plain silver ring one of our friends had made for me.

"I can't believe you still have it, that you still wear it."

He continued.

"Do you remember Rod Laver's book, 'How to Play Championship Tennis,' and how we took it to the courts with us?"

I didn't answer. I put my empty bottle down and I picked a fresh one off the table. I held my hands over the table to look at the old silver ring, the only ring I had ever worn.

Mine were not the hands of a teenage tennis player that we both used to be, or of someone who was a teaching pro in the years lived here. Now they were the hands of a functioning alcoholic with swollen fingers.

"I like most just to sit here by the dock with a beer in hand. I like to get a buzz on by the water."

They sat across from the multi-million-dollar homes of the rich who lived on the other side of the channel.

"She came with me the first time I came down here to live. When I left the tennis club we went back north and I started driving again. I was only here for two years. I got tired of teaching the older women. Some of them were OK players. Some of them didn't have enough to do, and were bored with their lives. I got bored with tennis too, with teaching, and with the people who had time to play tennis only because they did not have enough to do. Maybe if I had loved her, I would have felt differently about everything."

"Maybe I never really loved anyone."

The old tiki bar sat right on the water. There were docks next to the table where we sat so that you could bring your boat in from the river or the ocean or the intercoastal waterway. The outdoor bar was next to a small music stage where a band was getting ready to play.

"Do you know what a square grouper is?"

"No idea," he said.

"It's a kilo brick of marijuana that has fallen overboard."

"Arthur Ashe took the first match in three sets when he played against Ilie Năstase. Do you remember?" he asked.

"I don't remember a fucking thing about it. My memory's not too good sometimes. Like now. Maybe if I concentrate, I'll remember."

"And he took the last match against Țiriac in four sets."

"How the fuck do you remember this?"

"Clark Graebner was there, too. Remember him warming up Ashe for the first match? But Graebner didn't play in any of the matches the day we were there."

"Jesus Christ, I don't remember a fucking thing."

"I thought about it before we came here and looked it up. I thought you might remember since you continued to play and teach. You were a pro, I never was. It was senior year, and the only time we ever cut a class. You drove the old Biscayne because your brother wouldn't give you the TR3."

"You fucking got that right. I was a pro, and if I had entered that high school tournament, you never would have won that stupid little trophy!"

He grunted, the end of his cigarette burned brightly, and he looked over at me from the corner of his eyes. He just smiled at me and nodded.

"That's certainly possible," he responded, "but there's only one name on that stupid little trophy."

"That's exactly the kind of trophy it was," I laughed again, and so did he.

Long after so much of my life had failed, and disappointments in part of his as well, we sat together, two old friends from a childhood long ago and so much forgotten. We no longer rode bicycles, nor sat on street curbs to talk and watch the girls go by, nor played on the old broken-down tennis courts of our far away hometown. Now we sat in the shade on a sunny southern day at a tiny tiki bar, a beer in my hand, and a cigarette in his, smoke wafting over our table, and my swollen left hand wearing a small silver ring where the wedding band could have been so many years before. We all have failures, and at times we've had to surrender, but it's best to remember the victories.

At the Harold T. Clark Courts on a September day in 1969, the U.S. Davis Cup Team of Arthur Ashe, Stan Smith, and Bob Lutz defeated the Romanian team of Ilie Năstase and Ion Țiriac in twenty sets, five straight matches.

It is a victory my old friend had never forgotten.

Later, after I left the tiki bar, and managed to stumble my way back home alone to my own separate place, he went out onto his lanai. His wife of thirty some years entered the lanai to bring him a glass of wine, kissed him gently on the top of his head, and went back inside their home. He lit up another cigarette and sat back to remember our old friendship, the many years that had passed, and our once shared day of victory, as well.